MOONLIGHT KIN: AIDAN'S MATE

JORDAN SUMMERS

The last man Jenna Dane trusted betrayed her and stole everything she owned. She's been trying to get her 'life' back ever since. Her new job presents Jenna with the opportunity to recover what she's lost. All she has to do is betray Aidan Fortier and expose his secrets.

Secrets that could get her killed.

Aidan Fortier cannot allow a nosey human to snoop around his estate. He has a Werewolf pack to run, a full moon to contend with, and he must choose a mate. It would be a lot easier to do, if Jenna didn't smell so good. When trouble follows her to his doorstep, Aidan must decide whether to trust his Lycan instincts or throw Jenna to the wolves.

Dedicated to Bernard Lee DeLeo and Sasha White. Bernard, thank you for sharing your automotive expertise and lending me your eagle eyes. Anything I got wrong is entirely my fault. Sasha, thank you for not being afraid to tell me when something was wrong with the story. Your honesty is greatly appreciated and desperately needed in the world. I'd also like to thank Dar Dixon at Wicked Smart Designs for coming up with such a sexy cover.

CHAPTER ONE

The wolves stood in the clearing, their bodies quivering with a mixture of tension and excitement. The cool summer breeze wafted through the branches of the thick copse of trees, rustling the leaves.

Aidan Fortier stepped away from the group toward the center of the grass-covered clearing, his dark head held high. His gaze drifted over the assembled members of the pack. *His pack.* The wolves showed the proper respect by lowering their heads and dropping their gazes.

All but one.

René Dubois lost his wolf form and rose to his feet. Naked, he walked into the clearing until he stood a few yards from Aidan.

A big man and powerful wolf, René had more brawn than sense, which would be proven for the last time tonight. He'd openly disagreed with Aidan's decision to back his cousin, Damon's choice for a mate. René had considered the endorsement a betrayal of sorts, a sign that perhaps Aidan wasn't up to the task of running the pack.

René wasn't the only wolf who'd taken Aidan's decision as a sign of weakness. There'd been others who had voiced concerns, as was their right, but René was the only wolf that had come forward to present Aidan with a formal challenge for his position.

The brawny wolf wanted to be Alpha. Convinced his size would get him the coveted position. Tonight would determine who would rule the west coast Moonlight Kin pack.

Aidan had no intention of losing his Alpha position. He'd fought hard to get it and planned to keep it. The last few months aside, Aidan had done a good job of running the pack, both financially and politically.

But tonight wasn't about his money acumen or his diplomatic abilities. It wasn't even about the pack being in a better position now than they'd ever been. Tonight was about proving who was the strongest, fiercest, and most brutal male standing in this clearing. And the only way to do that was to fight to the death.

Aidan didn't relish the idea of killing René. He was a good man, a good wolf, and a productive pack member, but he'd never been the brightest bulb.

René was easily led, easily persuaded. Initially, Aidan wondered if that was why René had challenged him in the first place. Had he been goaded to act?

His gaze strayed to Robert LaBeouf. Aidan had absolutely no proof, other than a gut feeling, that his personal assistant was involved. Unfortunately, he couldn't present 'feelings' to the Lycanian Elders. They wanted evidence, especially when a charge carried a death sentence. Until Aidan found proof, he'd keep LaBeouf close.

Ultimately, the machinations behind the challenge didn't matter. Whatever or whoever was behind René stepping forward would mean nothing in the end. The challenge was issued and accepted. It could not be halted now.

Perhaps it was good that René had challenged him. The pack needed a reminder that despite his controversial decisions, he was still their leader and the most powerful wolf in the territory.

"A challenge for the position of Alpha has been issued by René Dubois and accepted by me," Aidan said. "As with all Alpha challenges, it will be a fight to the death. Does anyone have anything to add? To contest?"

Murmurs swept through the pack, but no one stepped forward.

"Very well then. Let's get this over with." Aidan shucked his clothes, dropping them carelessly onto the ground. Once he was naked, he turned to face René.

René slammed his meaty fists against his bare chest, then threw his head back and howled. Several of the wolves joined in until a chorus rang out.

Aidan waited, feeling no need to participate, since it was all for show. His wolf rose to the surface. Claws sprouted from his fingertips, replacing his blunted nails. Dull human teeth quickly became sharp incisors. His jaw stretched and grew until he sported a snout. It wasn't a complete change. That would come later once first blood was drawn.

René stopped howling and looked at him, his green eyes glowing in the darkness. Aidan nodded, then took a step back, so the big man could prepare for battle. René's body went through a partial shift, then he circled Aidan.

Aidan's claws clacked together in anticipation of René's attack. Despite being Alpha, it wasn't his place to strike first during a formal challenge. Had René chosen to go the informal route, then all bets would've been off.

The burly Were snorted as he stepped left, then right. At nearly six foot four, Aidan wasn't as big as René, but he made up for the difference with his speed and cunning. René growled and lunged at Aidan, his claws spread wide for the strike.

Aidan dodged and quickly whipped around to rake René's back. The Were hissed and jerked to the side, before Aidan could take off another strip from his hide. With first blood drawn, they both shifted the rest of the way.

René's body was still reshaping when Aidan launched himself onto the Were's back. He dug his claws into René's side and sank his teeth into his shoulder.

The Were twisted, getting a claw into Aidan's flank. He jerked his powerful arm and sent the Alpha flying through the air. Aidan crashed into the trunk of a tree, then quickly scrambled to his feet. René was strong. Incredibly strong. He shook his head to clear it and warily watched the Were, attempting to gauge his next move.

René quickly finished shifting, then charged him. Three hundred and some odd pounds of werewolf steamed toward Aidan.

He jumped to the side, but wasn't quick enough. René caught his shoulder and sent him sailing through low hanging branches. This time when Aidan looked up, there were two Renés standing in the clearing.

He blinked several times. The images wavered, then morphed into one. Aidan couldn't take another hit like that. The fur on his neck rose and he bared his teeth.

Aidan sat back on his haunches and launched himself at René. His claws caught the Were in the neck, taking them both down to the ground.

They rolled, snarling and growling, each trying to get the upper hand. Jaws snapped, as they tore out chunks of flesh. Aidan raked René with his claws, shredding fur and strips of skin.

Blood filled Aidan's mouth, fueling his instinct to go in for the kill. He ignored the pain searing his side, where René latched onto him. It was a desperate move, an attempt to get him to loosen his hold. Aidan refused to release him and bit down even harder.

René's gasps turned to strangled gurgles, as Aidan's jaws closed around his throat. The claws digging into Aidan's sides lost some of their intensity. Aidan shook his head and heard a distinctive *snap*. The Were's heavy mass slumped over him.

Aidan growled some more, then struggled to push René off him. The Were's lifeless body fell to the side. Sweat and blood covered Aidan from head to toe. As he rose, his body shifted into human form. He swayed, but somehow kept his feet beneath him.

"It is done," he gasped, his lungs bellowing. He glanced down at René. "If anyone else thinks that they can run the pack better than me, then say so now. Let it be known that I welcome all challenges, all discourse, but will not tolerate disloyalty."

Aidan walked over to where he'd left his clothes and dressed quickly. His head throbbed and the trees swayed before his eyes, but anyone looking at him would think that he was fine.

He made his way back to the house, wanting nothing more than to take a hot shower and crawl into bed. Aidan could still taste René's blood on his lips and feel it matting his hair.

What a waste.

The others would burn the Were's body and dispose of all his belongings. Tomorrow, he and the rest of the Moonlight Kin pack would celebrate René's life and mourn his death in the traditional Lycan way. The day after that, preparations would begin for the upcoming moon run.

* * * * *

CHAPTER TWO

Two Days Later...

The bed creaked as Aidan turned to nuzzle the plump breast beside his face. He inhaled deeply, taking in the deliciously ripe aroma of feminine heat.

Aidan's canines grew as he sucked the rosy nipple into his mouth and nipped at the sensitive nerve-endings, his tongue soothing the sting.

The dusky tip beaded eagerly in response, stabbing the roof of his mouth. A sensual moan came from the female beside him.

His ears perked. Aidan loved that sound. To him there was no greater sound on the planet, except perhaps a woman's cry of release, when he took her over the edge.

He swirled his tongue around her again, then leaned back to view his handiwork. The woman undulated, revealing more of her nakedness.

Beautiful, as only a female werewolf could be, she ran her sharp claws over her taught abdomen, then licked her lips and smiled.

Aidan grinned back, then threaded his hands into her long, red hair, successfully tangling his fingers. He used the silky strands to pull her closer, then captured her mouth in a blistering kiss. Their tongues tangled as they fed each other's passions.

Her ample body flooded in preparation for their joining. The woman's grip tightened around his neck. She moaned and her back bowed, crushing her breasts into his chest. Aidan's body tensed as his shaft hardened.

Was this it? Was she the one? He waited a beat, but felt *nothing*...beyond the usual physical pleasure.

Disappointed, he slowly released her lips.

Face flushed and panting for air, it took the woman a moment to recover her composure. She nudged his shoulder with her head, encouraging him to return. Her yellow-green eyes searched his longingly, even as her brow furrowed.

Aidan knew what she wanted. It was the same thing *all* the single females of the Moonlight Kin pack wanted when they came to his bed, but he couldn't force himself to take a bondmate. No amount of lust or sexual gymnastics would make it happen. Werewolf nature didn't work that way; though there were times he'd like it to be otherwise.

He stared at the gorgeous Were, her eyes still clouded with desire. Aidan couldn't deny the attraction sparking between them, but there'd be no love lost when they parted ways.

Her beauty and attentiveness didn't change the fact that this was nothing more than a chance at the lottery to her, a way to better her position in the pack. When she left his bed, there were fifteen others—literally—waiting to take her place.

Each more determined than the last to try her luck at becoming Alpha female of the west coast pack before the end of the moon run.

Unfortunately for this woman, sex held little interest to him now that his wolf had determined that she wasn't a match. His withdrawal made that obvious, but that wouldn't stop her from trying to *forge* a bond. They all tried.

Send her away, his wolf snarled.

The next female Were on the list currently waited down the hall in a small parlor for her chance to 'test' the Alpha. Aidan opened his mouth to tell this woman to leave, but stopped short when he spotted the determination in her lovely eyes.

"You are not my bondmate." The fact left no room for misunderstandings.

"I know," she said.

"If we do this, it means nothing." *Take the opportunity to back out gracefully.*

She shrugged. "I understand. I'd still like to…"

Did she understand?

Really?

Or was she simply hoping he was mistaken? As if such a thing were possible.

Aidan scrubbed a hand over his face. "As you wish." He'd fuck her like he did all the others, then send her back to the east wing, where she'd stay until the moon run next weekend.

Before he had a chance to act, the female Were hooked her foot around his leg to drag him closer.

Aidan growled, holding the urge to rut in check in order to remind her who was Alpha.

The woman immediately lowered her gaze and moved a small distance away. He would not allow any Werewoman to make demands upon him, especially one who wasn't his mate. It could lead to misunderstandings within the pack and unnecessary power struggles.

Aidan didn't play favorites. His wolves knew it, but that never stopped them from trying to change his mind.

To prove his point, Aidan rose out of the bed, leaving the woman tangled in the sheets. Naked, he strode across the room toward the French doors that led out to his balcony.

Not even a willing female in heat could hold his wolf's interest for long, once she'd been ruled out as a mate.

Aidan was beginning to believe nothing but his bondmate would satisfy his growing appetite and ease his restlessness. Years of searching and countless bedmates only added to his discontent.

Sex shouldn't be one long fucking audition, he thought.

A flash of gold caught his eye, stalling his hand on the door latch. His gaze wandered unerringly to the framed photo of the dark-haired child seated on his father's lap.

Two sets of amber eyes stared back at him, confirming that the wolf had bred true. Aidan's fingers hovered over the shiny frame. He drew his hand back, as if it had been singed.

Damon looked so damn happy holding his son. The toothy grin aimed at the camera would shame a Labrador.

Stupid pup, Aidan thought, then shook his head.

If he hadn't gone to the east coast to save his cousin's ass, Aidan was convinced that he wouldn't be suffering from this incessant longing for a mate now.

He'd succeeded in saving his cousin's life, but the act came at a steep cost. Damon had ended up bondmated to a female Hunter—a very *human* Hunter.

A fate worse than death in Aidan's mind. It was one thing to fuck one or accidentally eat one, but you didn't *bond* with humans and you certainly didn't convert them.

Technically, there were no Lycan laws against mating with a human, though Aidan had searched high and low to find one, convinced they should exist.

The best he and the other Lycanian Elders had come up with was an obscure reference in an ancient text that mentioned two instances of wolves successfully bonding with humans. Two, out of the thousands of years of Lycan history. Even Vegas wouldn't take those odds.

Aidan glanced at the woman in his bed, taking care to conceal his ambivalence. He'd spend a few useless hours with a Werewoman any day, if it meant avoiding Damon's fate.

Saddled to a human. He bristled. Never!

Damon's recklessness coupled with the added pressure from his fellow Elders cemented Aidan's resolve to remain true to the pack, true to his bloodline. Someone had to now that Damon had failed.

His gaze settled on the photograph once more. *Why did he have to look so damn happy?*

Something twinged inside of Aidan. Something he refused to acknowledge or name. Until he found his bondmate, there would be no smiling heirs for him.

Aidan growled and shoved the French doors open. They banged against the outside wall of the house, the glass panes rattling, as he stepped out onto the balcony, allowing the darkness to embrace him.

He inhaled to calm his racing heartbeat. The scent of pine trees surrounded him, their needles rustling in the mild summer breeze. The sharp tang mingled with the delicate aroma of the roses growing in his garden.

In the distance, he scented deer as they made their way through the woods, their silent hooves falling on the soft blanket of ferns below the green canopy.

Their careful efforts weren't enough to slip past the predator in him. Nothing came onto his property without him knowing about it, especially not prey.

Insects buzzed and frogs croaked in chorus, creating a symphony of night sounds. Their steady hum a soothing balm to his werewolf soul.

Aidan tilted his head toward the night sky and his blood pulsed, pulling him forward. The moon's gentle tug would turn into a riptide strong enough to yank his feet out from under him by the end of the week.

He closed his eyes and took a deep breath, his body shuddering with the urge to shift. Aidan threw his head back and let out a mournful howl, strangely diminished by his human form. Creatures scurried. Aidan's eyes opened and he scanned the tree-line. Instincts demanding that he give chase.

He turned away from the lure of the night and returned to

the warmth of his bed. No sense putting things off any longer, when there were others waiting.

"Last chance," he said. *Please go.*

"I want to stay." Her thick lashes concealed her emotions, but not the strength of her voice.

Aidan nodded. Without preamble, he dipped his fingers between her lush thighs, seeking her core. He stoked her, fueling her desire as he gathered the moisture needed to mount her. As soon as he had enough, Aidan climbed between her legs and thrust hard, entering her with one stroke.

He rode her relentlessly until she came, leaving her gasping and shuddering beneath him, then pulled out spilling his seed onto the sheets. Aidan rolled onto his side, his chest heaving.

"I'm sorry," he said.

"So am I." She rose quickly and pulled on her robe, then opened the door to leave.

Aidan's voice stopped her. "Send in the next woman."

Her mouth tightened and her shoulders tensed, but she managed to give him a clipped nod.

Tonight, like every night, he would sleep alone. That would remain the case until he located his bondmate or another Alpha managed to oust him from his position. Since the latter wasn't likely to happen anytime soon—thanks to René's recent challenge—Aidan would have to continue his search.

He closed his eyes and tried to imagine what it would be like, what she would be like. A soft knock on his bedroom door interrupted his thoughts.

"Enter," he said, reminding himself once again that this was his duty.

* * * * *

CHAPTER THREE

Aidan held the phone to his ear, listening to the other Lycanian Elders. They'd been droning on about his duties to his pack for an hour with no sign of the conference call coming to an end.

He lifted his cup of coffee and took a sip. Aidan grimaced. Cold. It had been hot, when his personal assistant brought it to him first thing this morning. Aidan put the cup back on his desk.

Robert LaBeouf knocked once and entered the library, which doubled as Aidan's office. His P.A.'s normally stony face sported a light blush and he wore a queer expression. Aidan held up one finger.

Robert nodded and kept his position by the door.

"I am well aware of my duties as Alpha," Aidan spoke into the receiver. "I do not need to be reminded again and again and again." He pinched the bridge of his nose to stave off a headache. "Yes, the women are here." Aidan took a deep breath to calm his temper. "No, I do not want to discuss my progress. If anything of import occurs, you all will be the first to know. Now I have to go." He disconnected the call before they could respond.

Robert stepped deeper into the room.

"What is it?" Aidan asked, grateful for any excuse to get off the phone.

"Sorry to bother you, Alpha," he said. "But we have a bit of a situation at the front gate."

Aidan tensed. "What kind of situation?" And why hadn't his wolves handled it already?

"We have a visitor." His normally monotone voice rose, belying his true emotions.

They never had visitors, unless the Lycanian Elders called a meeting or there was a moon run. Since he'd just got off the phone with the Elders and most of his pack was already here for the run, then that meant the visitor was a stranger.

"Hunter?" he asked.

His personal assistant shook his head. "Don't think so."

"Send them away." Aidan didn't have time to entertain any more guests. His house was already overflowing.

Robert's gaze darted back to the door. "I tried, Alpha, but she sat down in front of the gate and has refused to leave."

Aidan blinked in surprise. "She?" A sliver of premonition coursed through his veins, as he leaned against the edge of his desk. Aidan was careful not to disturb the neatly stacked papers he'd intended to read this morning, before the Lycanian Elders phoned and interrupted him.

"Yes, a human female, Sir." Robert nodded.

Human? Disappointment welled in Aidan's chest, though he didn't know why. It wasn't like he needed another female in his life right now. He gone through three Weres last night and still had thirteen to get through. "Send one of the wolves out," he said. "That should change her mind."

The crimson color in Robert's cheeks reached cartoonish levels. It took two tries for him to clear his throat. "That didn't work either," he said. "Byron came running back to the house with his tail tucked between his legs. He said that when the gate opened, he growled at her and she growled right back."

Aidan's brows rose. Either the woman was really brave, really stupid, or she was... "Are you sure that she's human?"

His assistant's gaze met his for a moment, then skittered away. "Once Byron came back, I went out to see for myself. There's no mistaking that *odor*."

Robert's disgust for humans was well known within the pack. He never bothered to hide his feelings about them, griping to anyone who'd listen. He thought they were all vermin that needed to be exterminated. Fortunately for humans, most *Weres* weren't so intolerant.

Aidan scratched his chin. "Did she say what she wanted?"

"She mentioned that her car broke down and that she needs to use a phone, but who doesn't have a cell phone these days?"

"Not many people," Aidan said. "It's possible that she has one, but it isn't charged."

"I suppose so. She certainly looks like someone who's been walking awhile. She's sweaty, but she doesn't smell right." Robert's nose wrinkled.

Aidan leaned forward. "What do you mean?"

"My senses tell me that there's more to her than meets the eye. I can't explain it, but I'm not convinced that her story isn't an elaborate trick to gain entrance to the residence. Humans can be so deceptive."

So could wolves, Aidan thought, eyeing the man.

The woman's arrival could be a ruse. It wasn't out of the realms of possibility. His success in business dealings had garnered an unusual amount of attention—unwanted attention, considering the secrets Aidan kept. Reporters phoned constantly. Everyone wanted an exclusive from the famous software *recluse*.

If the woman was a reporter, she'd regret this bold move. No one came to his house uninvited. By the time Aidan finished with her, she'd be so frightened that she'd leave the area.

Of course, if she were as she said—a stranded motorist, he couldn't exactly leave her out there to wander around unsupervised. Aidan could not afford for her, or anyone else, to be traipsing around the estate this close to the full moon.

"Show her in." Aidan already regretted his decision, but at least he'd know if she were lying.

Robert's gaze shot to his face and his eyes widened. "Alpha?"

"You heard me."

"But she seems dangerous," Robert said.

Aidan pressed his lips together to keep from laughing. "I'm sure that a pack of werewolves can handle one human female. Don't you?"

"Yes, sir. Of course, but it can't hurt to keep an eye on her." Robert left, pulling the door closed behind him.

Aidan shook his head. He had no doubt Robert would keep watch, waiting for the unsuspecting human to cross the line, so he could invoke Lycan law.

Robert would use any excuse to kill one of them. Luckily, he needed permission to do so and Aidan wasn't likely to grant it.

He glanced at the phone on his desk. He should've called the authorities to have the woman removed for trespassing. That was the prudent thing to do, but Aidan couldn't shake his curiosity.

What type of woman growled at a wolf?

The same type who was foolish enough to come here on their own.

Aidan stepped in front of the antique mirror on the wall to inspect his appearance. His unfashionably long black hair fell past his shoulders in desperate need of a cut. He checked his teeth to make sure there wasn't raw meat stuck in them.

The move stretched and twisted the jagged white scar that ran across his chin, cutting into his otherwise polished appearance. He ran his finger over the thin line, admiring the memento he'd gotten the night he became Alpha.

Sharp amber eyes stared back from the mirror. In a few more days, they'd begin to glow and the façade he presented to the human world would disappear. His beast would rise and Aidan would be more instinct than man.

He smiled in anticipation of the full moon and the freedom it brought him. A knock sounded on the door as he turned away from the mirror. "Enter."

Robert poked his head in. "I've put her in the parlor."

Aidan gave him a curt nod, then walked out of the library across the marbled entry hall to the closed door on the opposite side. Aidan raised his hand to knock, stopping short in surprise, unsure why he found the need to do so in his own home.

He frowned and turned the knob. This was his house. He damn well didn't need to announce himself. Aidan entered the parlor, his footsteps silent on the hardwood floor.

The woman's back was to him, her slender frame partially obscured by the cascade of strawberry blond ringlets flowing over her narrow shoulders and down her back. A worn camouflage bag lay at her feet.

Aidan's gaze locked onto her heart-shaped bottom as it swayed to some internal beat. Her long legs were bare where her brown walking shorts left off. Strong thighs, made for grasping a man's waist, flexed with each side-to-side motion.

A wisp of bare abdomen peeked out beneath a short white cotton shirt. Aidan couldn't see her breasts or her face, but it didn't matter. She already had his undivided attention.

He inhaled to get a read on her before she had a chance to open her mouth and lie. The scent of lilacs in the spring slammed into him.

Aidan scanned the parlor to ensure that Robert hadn't placed a bouquet in the room. He hadn't. *She* was the source of the delicious aroma.

She bent over to get a better look at the photos in the

curio cabinet. The move caused the material of her shorts to pull tight and cup her bottom. Aidan's mouth watered and a rumble came from his chest.

The woman gasped and spun around, knocking the lamp off the end table in the process. She fumbled to catch the base, but missed.

Aidan rushed forward, using his preternatural speed, and caught the lamp before it shattered on the ground. When he looked up, their eyes met and the breath froze in his lungs.

The woman had the face of a road-weary angel, who'd taken flight one too many times. Wide ice-green eyes, the color of pale peridot, watched him in shocked silence. A strong chin supported full lips that dipped and swelled, all but begging to be kissed.

Those same luscious lips parted, breaking into a lopsided grin. That silly smile drew attention to the freckles dotting her high cheekbones and pert little nose. That same nose crinkled, as he continued his undisguised perusal.

"I'm Jenna." She scrubbed her hand on the side of her shorts, then held it out for him to shake.

"Aidan." For a second or two, he simply stared at her, unable to move, then ever so gently he clasped his big hand around her smaller one.

The jolt hit like a shock from a wet plug.

Aidan's jaw clenched, as part of his body inconveniently stirred to life. He forced himself to release her, then pulled his shirt down to hide his perplexing condition. Aidan opened and closed his hand to dispel the remaining tingles.

A single curl dropped onto her forehead. Jenna tucked the stray behind her ear, exposing an angry purple slash that bisected part of her eyebrow. Although he could see no blood, the wound smelled fresh.

"Did you have an accident?" he asked. "My assistant was under the impression that your car broke down."

"It did," she said. *Truth. Lie.* No wonder his wolves were having such a difficult time reading her.

"The wound on your eyebrow says differently." His voice chilled the air around them.

Jenna's hand flew up to cover the area. Her smile faded. Her clear bright eyes dimmed, overshadowed by wariness.

Aidan sniffed, scenting her again.

Underneath the sweet aroma of lilacs a faint odor of a man's cheap cologne lingered on her clothes. His thoughts took a dark turn. Was he the one who'd struck her?

A growl came from his throat. Aidan coughed twice to cover up the unbidden noise. The urge to shake her until she told him everything about this man besieged him. He clenched his fists at his sides to keep from acting on the impulse.

She's human. A stranger. And most definitely not his responsibility.

Aidan fought to regain control of his turbulent emotions. His mind flashed to the hearing he'd attended on Damon's behalf. His cousin had professed his love for the human woman, his bondmate. He'd said there was no denying the wolf once it made up its mind.

A buzzing noise sounded in Aidan's head, before being drowned out by his own heart beat thundering in his chest.

Well it wasn't going to happen to him, damn it. He was a Lycanian Elder. He had responsibilities. He didn't think with his dick.

Aidan ignored the strange feelings of possession that had momentarily overwhelmed him. It was just the pull of the full moon and his instinctual need to protect everything in his territory. It had to be.

The fact the woman was human was coincidental.

* * * * *

Jenna had sensed his presence a moment before he'd cleared his throat. She'd turned too quickly and lost her balance, knocking an expensive looking lamp off the end table.

He'd moved with incredible speed, catching the fixture before it hit the floor.

When Jenna had looked up, an unusual pair of amber eyes had immediately captured her. The warm honey hue had heated and cooled as the man assessed her. His eye color was made all the more striking due to the contrast to his ebony hair. Jenna normally didn't like guys with long hair, but for some reason the style suited him.

She'd actually felt her heart skip a beat. Jenna thought that kind of thing only happened in fiction, not real life. Of course, men that looked like him didn't exist in real life either. Yet here he was, standing in front of her.

Never in all her years had she ever seen a man so devastatingly handsome. Nothing, not even the scar on his chin, could detract from his perfectly chiseled features. It was the one blemish that stood between him and the definition of pretty.

Her heart tripped again. Once could be dismissed as coincidence, but twice pointed to attraction.

Jenna had given up on being attracted to any man after her ex-boyfriend, Ethan Manning's betrayal three months ago, so to find herself drawn to this man, this stranger was disconcerting.

Muscles rippled beneath his form-fitting shirt, as he lifted the lamp and gently set it back onto the table. Power oozed from his pores. Not the kind of power that Ethan flaunted, but a more subtle strength that he wielded like it was his birthright. At no point did he look away.

The room shrank around them, cocooning them in a fragile bubble that one wrong word would pop.

As he straightened to his full height, Jenna had to crane her neck to maintain eye contact. She'd murmured her name or at least she hoped that she had. He'd responded in kind.

Aidan…

It was the kind of name that swirled on your tongue and

bore repeating. She swayed toward him, sucked in by the odd gravitational pull happening between them. The second Jenna noticed that she'd moved closer, her face flamed and she stepped back.

What was wrong with her? Had she learned nothing in the last few months?

Jenna swallowed hard. "Sorry about the lamp."

He remained silent.

She fidgeted. "Thank you for letting me in to use your phone."

Amusement lit his amber eyes. "You didn't give me much choice." He watched her closely.

Oops! She hadn't, had she?

Jenna had already apologized. What else was there to say or do? "Sooner I use your phone, the sooner I'll be out of your hair."

Aidan pointed to the phone on the desk. "What about your car?" he asked.

Jenna tensed. No way could she afford a tow truck. It would cost a fortune to get the Bug to Breakbend. If she had her garage handy, this wouldn't be a problem. But thanks to her conniving ex, she didn't.

Ethan had taken the only thing of value she'd ever owned, the only place she'd ever called home, and the only family she'd ever known. And for what? So he could build a stupid luxury condominium complex? Like the world needed another one of those.

Jenna gritted her teeth. "I'll get the car when I can."

* * * * *

Her scent soured at the mention of her vehicle. Aidan watched her dig into her pocket and pull out a crumpled piece of paper with a number scribbled on it. Jenna picked up the phone and punched in the number. She tapped her fingers against the desk as she waited for someone to answer.

He heard a woman come on the line.

"May I please speak with Paul Welling?" Jenna asked.

Sirens went off in his head. Aidan instantly recognized the name of the Gazette editor. Had Robert been right about her all along?

"Hi, Mr. Welling. It's Jenna Dane."

"Jenna, where have you been?" he asked. "I expected you here hours ago."

"I ran into car trouble."

"Where are you?" he sounded dubious.

"I'm not sure." Jenna looked at Aidan and mouthed *'Where am I'*?

Aidan blinked. She didn't know? How could she not know? "The Fortier estate," he said casually, waiting for some sign of recognition to cross her face. None came. Jenna stared blankly at him. She had no idea who he was. Aidan's tension eased a notch.

"I'm outside of town," she said.

"If you're not here in the next two hours, don't bother coming," Paul said.

Jenna turned her back to Aidan and whispered into the phone, though she needn't have bothered. Aidan had been listening to both sides of the conversation and didn't feel an ounce of guilt about eavesdropping.

"Please, Mr. Welling. I need this job." Her desperation was palpable.

For some reason, Aidan found himself responding to it, to her.

He slipped out of the room and summoned Robert. "Take Nic and go find her car."

"What do you want us to do with it once we find it?" he asked.

"Bring it to me. Something is off about her and I want to know what it is. In the meantime, have the Range Rover brought around to the front of the house. She needs transportation."

Robert gaped. "You're going to give the Rover to a human?"

His hackles rose. "Yes, do you have a problem with that?"

Robert's gaze dropped. "No, sir."

"Good." Aidan strolled back into the room in time to see Jenna wipe moisture from her face. The tears clinging to her eyelashes were the only evidence that remained to prove she'd been crying.

She gave him a strained smile. "Thanks for the use of the phone."

"Anytime," Aidan heard himself say.

Jenna hoisted her bag onto her shoulder and walked to the door. Her hand hesitated on the knob. "I know it's rude of me to ask, but you wouldn't happen to have any tools I can borrow, would you?"

"Tools?" What in the world did she need with tools?

"Yeah, socket wrenches, pliers, things like that? I'll give them back. I promise."

Intrigued by the request, Aidan asked, "What do you need them for?"

"I thought maybe I could fix Stan," she said.

"Stan?" *Who was Stan? And why was he just hearing about him?* Unexpected anger flared inside of Aidan.

Jenna laughed, oblivious to his mood change. "Stan is my car."

Aidan's brow quirked. "You have a name for your car?"

She shrugged. "Don't you? I thought all guys did."

His eyes scrolled over the front of her T-shirt, taking in the soft slope of her full breasts. Aidan watched her nipples harden and tore his gaze away. "You are most definitely not a man," he said in a garbled voice.

Jenna crossed her arms over her chest. "I know, but it doesn't stop me from naming cars—or fixing them."

"You're a mechanic?" He'd assumed she was a reporter.

"I used to be." She bit her lip and looked away.

His gaze was drawn to her mouth like a lodestone. Oh, the things he could do with those lips. The part of his body he refused to acknowledge, twitched behind his zipper.

Aidan shook his head to clear it. What was wrong with him? He shouldn't be thinking about her mouth or how her body responded to him. She was human. He shouldn't be thinking about her at all.

Jenna stared at him. "Do you have the tools or not?"

Robert knocked on the door and stepped into the room. He scowled at Jenna, then handed the keys to Aidan and left.

"You only have two hours to reach town. There's no time to fix your vehicle."

"How did you know about—?"

"Take these." He handed her the keys to the Range Rover, effectively cutting off a question he could not answer. "My *men* will retrieve your car."

Jenna reached for the keys automatically. "You don't have to do that."

"I insist." Aidan dropped them into her hand. "I'll have your car repaired."

"No!" she snapped. "I mean it's not necessary. You've done too much already. I can fix it myself."

Was she in trouble or was she worried about getting caught in a lie?

Aidan opened his mouth to tell her that he'd do as he damn well pleased, but stopped when he glimpsed the panic in her eyes. "There's a garage on the estate. I'm sure you'll find everything you need there," he said instead.

"But…"

He held up his hand. "No arguments. Your car will be there tomorrow." What was he doing? Aidan had obviously lost his mind. Her and her stupid lilac scent was making him crazy. "I'll show you to the front door.

Aidan practically shoved her out of the room and down the hall. He needed to get Jenna away from his home and out of his head.

Jenna trotted to keep up, but said nothing more. She climbed into the Rover, then turned to thank him again.

Aidan didn't give her the chance. He spun on his heel, and like prey evading a predator, bolted for the front door.

*****

CHAPTER FOUR

The drive to Breakbend took longer than Jenna thought. She'd overestimated the distance she'd driven and would never have made it to her new job by the end of the day had she continued walking.

Jenna kept watch in the rearview mirror for any sign of Carl Rich. She might've changed vehicles, but she couldn't afford to underestimate the private investigator her swindling ex had hired to find her. The man was doggedly persistent.

Of course with millions riding upon obtaining her signature, Jenna wasn't surprised. That kind of money would motivate anyone.

Her fingers brushed the healing gash over her eyebrow and she winced. The wound reminded her just how close Carl had come to capturing her a week ago. She'd barely escaped his grasp. Jenna didn't think she'd be as lucky next time.

Carl had learned the hard way that she wasn't a victim. She got some satisfaction from knowing that her swift kick had landed squarely in Carl's crotch. If there was any justice in the world, his balls still ached.

Breakbend trickled into view. Trees slowly gave way to

frontier storefronts and trendy coffee shops. Some of the buildings looked original, but most were manufactured to appear 'old'.

A few high-end restaurants stood out amongst the mom and pop establishments, along with the usual array of fast food chains that invaded every town.

Two billboards advertised a nearby lake that touted great fishing. The lake appeared to be Breakbend's only claim to fame.

The Breakbend Gazette had pride of place on the main drag, between a diner and a jewelry shop. She spotted a car pulling out of a space in front of the paper and quickly slid the Rover into the vacated spot.

Jenna checked her appearance in the rearview mirror. If she'd been going for the deranged lion with mascara issues look, she'd be set. Unfortunately, she'd been going for 'urban professional', which wasn't going to happen today. On the bright side, at least she'd stopped sweating.

She fixed her face the best she could and rearranged her hair to hide the cut above her eyebrow, then killed the engine. Jenna took a deep breath, then climbed out of the SUV. A bell clanged as she pushed the door open to the Breakbend Gazette.

A receptionist sat near the entrance, filing her nails. Her orange floral print dress accentuated her wide hips and generous belly, while leaching color from her peachy complexion. A brown bob haircut stopped at her jawline, exposing her double chins.

Her strategic position guarded the spattering of worn desks beyond. Most were empty, but a few still held what Jenna assumed were reporters. They varied in age from pimple-faced to geriatric.

Jenna approached her desk.

The receptionist wrinkled her nose. "Can I help you?"

Jenna straightened the front of her sweat-stained shirt and brushed a stray curl behind her ear. The woman's gaze shot to the bruised cut by her eyebrow.

"I had an accident," Jenna said.

The woman's gaze softened. "I understand."

No, she didn't. No one could comprehend the hell Jenna had gone through these past three months.

"Mr. Welling is expecting me."

"Name?" she asked.

"Jenna Dane."

The receptionist's eyes widened and her face transformed once more. "I'm Molly. Molly Jones." She held out her hand. "Nice to meet you. Welcome to the Breakbend Gazette," she said, then swiveled her chair around and shouted toward a closed office door at the back of the small space. "Paul! Jenna's here."

The door flew open, hitting the wall with a loud bang. "Molly, how many times have I told you not to shout for me? It's unprofessional. Why do you think I installed that fancy phone system?" The closer Paul Welling got, the more rumpled he appeared. His suit had been new…in the seventies, along with his haircut.

Jenna stepped forward to introduce herself.

"It's about time you got here." He ignored her outstretched hand.

"Sorry." Jenna dropped her arm. "I had car trouble."

"Nice car." Molly stared at the Range Rover, a devilish gleam in her eye. "Wish I had that kind of trouble."

So it was going to be like that, Jenna thought. Her lips thinned, but she didn't say anything to Molly. She couldn't afford to lose this job.

Reporting for the Gazette was her big chance—her last chance to earn enough money to hire an attorney to fight Ethan.

"It's not mine," Jenna said.

"Whose is it?" Paul's brown eyes narrowed. "I was under the impression that you were new to the area. If I find out that you're lying to me, then you're fired."

"I'm not. I've never been to Breakbend." She'd never even heard of the town before answering the ad. "I broke down near the Fortier estate. A man named Aidan loaned me the SUV, until I can get my car repaired."

Molly gasped. Everyone in the room stopped what they were doing and stared at Jenna.

She flustered. "What?"

"Aidan Fortier?" Molly asked.

"I don't know," Jenna said. "I didn't catch his last name."

"Who else could it be?" Molly asked Paul.

"There's only one Aidan in the area," he said.

Molly shook her head. "I can't believe he let you inside the estate."

Jenna was confused. "Why wouldn't he?"

Molly glared at her. "He never lets anyone in, aside from his employees. He's very secretive."

Maybe no one had tried sitting in front of his gate and refusing to move. Jenna almost smiled as she recalled the look on everyone's face, when she'd done so. Aidan hadn't exactly rolled out the welcome mat, but he had helped her. In Jenna's book, that counted for a lot.

"Is it true that he has wolf packs running around his property?" Molly asked.

Jenna had seen one wolf, but not a pack. She decided to keep that information to herself. "Is he part of some kind of weird cult?"

Molly waved her question aside. "No, nothing like that. He's just peculiar."

One of the male reporters came over to where they stood. "I heard he was horribly disfigured and that's why he's rarely seen in public."

Jenna frowned. "Are we still talking about Aidan?" They couldn't be referring to the gorgeous man she'd met.

"Duh." Molly rolled her eyes, as if she were dense. "Is it true he runs around in robes and has a harem?"

Jenna snorted. "Where are you guys getting your

information from?" Aidan had gone from eccentric wolf whisperer to a sheik in seconds.

"Don't laugh." Molly grabbed her arm. "There are tons of rumors surrounding Aidan Fortier. Some people in these parts don't think he's human. They say he howls at the moon with his wolves."

The male reporter nodded in agreement. Paul Welling watched Jenna. She assumed he did so to see how she'd react.

"You're kidding, right?"

"It's no joke," the male reporter said.

Coming to Breakbend was obviously a mistake. These people were crazy. "You honestly believe Aidan's a werewolf?"

"Don't be ridiculous," Molly said earnestly. "He's probably a vampire. These parts attract creatures of the night."

Jenna waited for her to laugh.

Molly didn't.

She looked at all the somber faces in the room. This had to be a prank. Why weren't they laughing? They couldn't all be delusional. Could they?

Fear prickled the skin at the base of her neck. Jenna needed to defuse this situation before it got worse. If they honestly believed Aidan was some kind of monster, how long would it be before they convinced themselves that he should be hunted down and destroyed?

"I assure you, Aidan's as human as you or I." Jenna extracted her arm from Molly's grasp. She hoped whatever had made them crazy wasn't catching.

"Come into my office," Paul said. "I'll get you your paperwork and explain everything."

Jenna followed Paul Welling to the back of the small space. If anything, his office was even more dingy than the outer area.

A scratched wooden desk sat in the center of the room.

Piles of papers and a laptop covered much of the surface. An old office chair missing half of its padding rested behind the desk, while two folding chairs faced the front of it.

"Take a seat." Paul pointed to one of the folding chairs.

Jenna perched on the edge of one, but didn't settle in. She was afraid to after everything they'd said to her. How could these people believe all the crazy stories circulating about Aidan? Weren't newspapers supposed to deal in facts?

Paul typed a few keys on his laptop, then turned the screen toward her. "See this?"

Jenna frowned. "What am I looking at?"

"That's all the information the world has on Aidan Fortier," he said. "Pretty interesting given he's a multi-millionaire, isn't it?"

"Not really. It's common for wealthy people to keep a low profile for security reasons." It was obvious Aidan had money. People didn't get to live on a fortified estate without it. "Have you ever thought that maybe he likes his privacy? I know it's a rarity in this world, but it does still occur on occasion."

"Oh, I'm sure he does." Paul made it sound as if Aidan's wishes were of no consequence. "The question is why?"

"I'm sure there are a multitude of reasons," she said.

"Do you have any idea what an exclusive interview with the famous software developing recluse would fetch? A lot!" he said, before she could answer. "If we can't get an interview, I'd settle for something scandalous like a photo of him howling at the moon."

Oh, is that all?

She inched forward. "Do you really believe he's a werewolf?"

"Recluse, eccentric, werewolf, vampire, I don't care what he is, as long as it helps me sell papers."

Okey, dokey. Jenna's lips thinned. She didn't like the direction this conversation was taking.

"One page on Aidan Fortier would get us both out of this

town and into the journalistic big leagues," he said.

Jenna didn't care about the 'big leagues'. All she wanted was to earn enough money to give Ethan a good legal fight.

"I didn't come here to write gossip pieces or fiction. Had I known that you'd have me looking for Bigfoot on my first day, I wouldn't have bothered to apply for the job."

"Aidan Fortier isn't Bigfoot," Paul said.

"Well he sure as heck isn't a werewolf!" Jenna snapped. "What someone does with their spare time is none of our business, as long as they aren't harming anyone."

She had experienced firsthand what lies and sensationalism could do to someone's reputation. That had been the first blow Ethan Manning had struck after cheating her out of her garage.

Instead of a David meets Goliath story, the press had sided with her ex and made her out to be a lying, thieving, gold-digger. Customers stopped bringing their cars in for repair long before Ethan put locks and chains on the doors.

Jenna had managed to hang onto the land the garage had been built on, but if she didn't get legal help soon, she'd lose it, too.

"How dedicated are you to this job?" Paul asked.

"What do you mean?" Jenna didn't have enough cash to leave town.

"I hired you, even though technically you didn't have enough experience."

"Thank you again for giving me a chance." It pained her to say those words.

Paul sneered. "I don't want your thanks. I want you to get an interview with Aidan Fortier or some information about his private life. If you do that, it would go a long way toward proving to me that you are committed. That you deserve this job," he said. "I'd hate to think that I'd made a mistake by giving you the position."

"You haven't."

"Then prove it!" He bellowed. "Reporting isn't about

being nice. It's about uncovering the truth."

Jenna's eyes narrowed. "You're not talking about the truth. You're talking about sensationalism and possible libel."

Paul leaned forward. "The truth comes in many forms. Some just pay better than others."

Jenna's stomach knotted. Manipulating the facts to accommodate an agenda wasn't her idea of journalism. And ultimately that's what Paul was asking her to do.

Any other time, she'd tell him to stick this job up his butt, but Jenna was down to her last fifty and pride wouldn't buy food or gas. Still, she didn't like the idea of taking advantage of someone who'd shown her kindness.

"I'll give it some thought." She choked on the words as they lodged in her throat.

"You do that." Paul gave her a knowing glance. "I expect you to report back to me in the morning with your answer."

Jenna left his office, nausea replacing her earlier hunger. Molly stood nearby, casually flicking through back issues of the Gazette. The second Jenna appeared she pounced.

"So what's he like?" Molly asked.

"Paul?"

Molly frowned. "No, Aidan," she said. "Everyone knows that Paul is an asshole."

"I heard that, Molly," he said.

"Knew you would," she said.

Jenna sighed. At least that was one thing they could agree upon. "Aidan seemed like any other mega successful business man. Slightly aloof. Cultured. Intense." And way too sexy for his own good.

There it was again. That unbidden attraction that cropped up every time she thought about the man.

"What does he look like?" Molly asked.

Jenna shrugged. "Dark hair. Longish. Tall."

"You're going to have to do better than that, if you're going to work for my parents' paper. People like description," she said.

Well that explained why Molly could do or say whatever she wanted. If her folks owned the paper, she had no fear of getting fired.

Molly clasped her hands against her chest. "What's his body like? Is he fit? Fat? Thin? Somewhere in between?"

Jenna pictured Aidan's wide shoulders and flat stomach. Fit didn't begin to describe his banging body. Something inside her fluttered. Something she promptly squashed before it could take form.

"Don't keep me in suspense," Molly whined.

Jenna cleared her suddenly dry throat. "Yeah, he's in good shape."

"I knew it!" She grinned. "He sounds dreamy."

"I hadn't noticed," Jenna lied. For some reason, it bothered her that Molly was so interested in Aidan. It shouldn't matter. It wasn't like she and Aidan had any connection beyond his vehicle. "I'll see you tomorrow." Jenna rushed to the door, hoping she didn't follow.

"Where are you going?" Molly asked.

"To my motel. I'm beat." The lie slipped easily from Jenna's lips. She couldn't exactly say that she planned to sleep in the SUV. Businesses rarely employed homeless people.

She left quickly before Molly could ask any more questions. The little bell chimed loudly behind her as she stepped onto the sidewalk. Jenna sucked in the fresh air to clean the mental filth Paul had left in her mind. She walked, needing to get away.

Maybe you had to be scheming or insane to do the job. If that were the case, Jenna wouldn't last long.

She found a fast food restaurant to dine in and used their bathroom to get cleaned up. Jenna got a few strange looks when she came out of the restroom with a wet head, but no one said anything.

She waited until the Gazette closed, then walked back to

the Rover. Jenna studied the navigation system to see what was around.

A campground located five miles down the road looked like her best bet. They tended to be cheap and rarely asked questions.

Jenna drove in silence, her body and mind weary from the day's events. She put aside Molly's ridiculous ideas and thought about everything Paul Welling had told her.

Was it true that an interview with Aidan could fetch big money? Could she afford to pass up the opportunity, if there was even a remote chance that was the case?

The truth was no, she could not. Paul might be willing to settle for something scandalous about Aidan, but Jenna wouldn't. She couldn't. And she prayed that her desperation never reached that point.

Jenna pulled into the campground and found an out-of-the-way spot to park and settle in for the night. She grabbed a jacket from her tote, then climbed into the backseat.

With a click of a button, Jenna locked the doors, then tried to get comfortable. The Rover had a lot more space in the backseat than the Bug, which was probably why she found it so difficult.

She was used to being cramped. The tight fit made her feel protected, even though it was an illusion. Jenna plucked a shirt out of her bag and rolled it up, creating a makeshift pillow.

Thanks to Molly's ravings and Paul's veiled threats, sleep didn't come easily.

* * * * *

Aidan couldn't get Jenna out of his mind. Her lilac scent lingered in the parlor and clung to his skin. He shook his head and snorted, but it did little to alleviate the aroma.

He walked into Robert's office. "I'm going to my room to grab a shower. Send up the next Were on the list," he said, more gruffly than he'd intended.

Robert nodded. "Right away."

Hair still damp, Aidan stood on his balcony inhaling the night, while he waited for the woman to arrive.

There was a soft knock at the door.

"Come in," he said without turning around. He heard the woman enter the room.

"Alpha, you called for me." Her sultry voice whispered over his skin.

Aidan tore his gaze away from the view of the backyard. Golden hair framed a narrow face, making her skin glow. A blue silk robe did little to conceal her lush curves. Aidan held out his hand.

"Come here, Sydney," he said.

She strolled across the room, her hips swaying teasingly with each step. When she was within arm's length, she reached out and placed her fingers into his hand, allowing him to pull her into his arms.

Soft breasts met his hard chest and Aidan inhaled. Sydney's warm scent tickled his nose. She smelled buttery like fresh baked bread—and all wrong. Aidan inhaled her delicious scent again. This time he sneezed, wrinkling his nose.

"Bless you," Sydney said in surprise.

"Thank you."

She rubbed her hand over his chest, trailing her fingers down until she found his soft shaft. Sydney stroked him, then waited for a response. There was none. She ran her palm over his length again and squeezed.

Aidan's cock twitched, but remained flaccid. Fear crept from his gut to his head, leaving tension in its wake. He took an awkward step back. This had *never* happened before.

He'd been with three women yesterday and hadn't experienced any problems. Maybe that was it. Maybe he'd overdone it yesterday. Or maybe he was ill. But even as the thought whispered through his head, Aidan knew that wasn't the case.

Werewolves didn't get sick and they certainly didn't have performance issues. Their hormones ran hot year around.

Aidan cursed under his breath and glanced down at his limp dick. *What the hell is the matter with you?*

Sydney took a step back. "Alpha?"

"I've changed my mind," he said. "I want you to leave. Now!"

Her face reddened. "I understand."

Aidan gritted his teeth. "You understand nothing." How could she, when he didn't understand what was happening? "Go!"

Sydney rushed to the door and slipped out of the room, before he could say another word. No doubt she'd report his 'condition' to the others.

Aidan swore again. This was the last thing he needed. *First his cousin, then the challenge, now this.* Aidan's chest squeezed. He needed to get outside. He couldn't breathe.

He shed his clothes and leapt off his balcony, transforming into a massive black wolf in mid-air. With silent paws, Aidan landed on the grass and took off running for the trees.

He ran hard, until exhaustion took him.

No longer on estate property, Aidan loped through the woods, searching for a place to bed down for the night. He couldn't bear to return to his room. He wasn't ready to face the shame or the failure.

He settled on a spot in the park under a canopy of trees, not far from a campground. Aidan scented the area for danger one final time, then dropped down onto the soft ferns. For a moment, he thought he smelled lilacs. First his body, now his nose was betraying him. He shook his head in disgust, then rested his muzzle upon his paws.

Aidan slept fitfully, dreams of curly, strawberry blond hair and the smell of fresh lilacs, haunting him until dawn.

* * * * *

Through the thick trees, in a secluded campsite nearby, Jenna tossed and turned in the backseat of the Range Rover. For the first time in three months, Ethan Manning wasn't taking center stage in her dreams. He'd been replaced by a dark-haired demon with amber eyes, whose smile could quite literally melt the clothes off any woman.

* * * * *

CHAPTER FIVE

Ethan Manning nodded patiently at the bloated banker sitting across from him. On the outside Ethan appeared calm, but inside, his anger roiled, churning with the need to smash something.

"You have until Monday," the banker said. "After that, we'll have no choice, but to remove our offer."

"I need more time," Ethan smiled through clenched teeth. Only a fool would mistake it for a friendly grin. How much cash had his family stored within those re-enforced walls? How many investments had they made?

Too many to count. Certainly enough to afford him some leeway and keep the banker in thousand dollar suits for the rest of his life.

The pompous ass straightened his food-stained tie and squinted against the setting sun. "We've already extended the deadline twice in deference to your family, but we cannot extend it again. We have a board of trustees to answer to and other investments to consider. You understand."

Ethan understood all right. If he didn't get his hands on Jenna Dane soon, he'd lose more than his initial investment. He'd leveraged over half of his inheritance on this land deal.

He wouldn't be *poor* by most people's standards, but by Manning family standards he might as well be destitute.

This was the type of business blunder that tarnished family names. Something his father and mother would not tolerate—not even from their son.

It was a good thing the private detective he'd hired had found Jenna Dane. Ethan didn't want to think about if he hadn't.

The banker rose and extended his hand. Ethan glared at it until the man slowly brought it back to his side. He grabbed the glasses perched on his nose and carefully wiped them with a handkerchief. "I'll expect to hear from you before the deadline." He placed his glasses back on and walked to the door.

Ethan watched him leave, then picked up the crystal candy dish on his desk and hurled it toward the wall. The dish exploded on impact, raining multi-colored mints and shiny glass shards onto the Persian rug. No one was going to fuck up this deal for him, especially not a low-class, second-rate mechanic.

He needed to find out exactly where they were. Carl and Jenna should've arrived in town by now. Ethan glanced at his calendar. Had it been a week since they last spoke?

That couldn't be right.

It didn't take a week to drive back to Vancouver. He waited to get his temper in check, then buzzed his executive assistant. "Cynthia, get me Carl Rich on the phone."

"Right away, Mr. Manning."

A moment later the phone rang. Ethan picked it up and without preliminaries said, "Where is she?"

There was a pause, then Carl's gruff voice said, "I lost her, but I have a couple of leads to follow up on."

"What do you mean you lost her? The last time we spoke you'd found her and had Jenna in your custody. You told me that you were on your way." Ethan clutched the receiver, his knuckles white. "What the hell happened? I expected you to be here by now." Something akin to panic clawed at his chest until he could barely breathe.

"She's pretty resourceful when she needs to be. She gave me the slip at a gas station, when I stopped to fill up," he said. "Hitchhiked back to her car and disappeared."

Fury over the man's incompetence made his shake. "How did a woman give you the slip? I thought you were a professional."

"She's tougher than she looks and obviously very persuasive when she needs to be," Carl ground out.

Ethan was beginning to understand that about Jenna. Somehow she'd eluded them for three months, but her admirable survival skills didn't change his objective. He'd paid a lot of money and expected results.

"I don't pay you for excuses," Ethan said. "Find her now or you won't see another dime. And just so we're clear, if you fail me again, I'll have your license yanked. You won't be able to get a job parking cars in this town. Got it?"

"Understood." The word was ripped from his throat. "Trust me, sir. She will not get away again," he said with menacing promise.

"Call me the second you spot her. I want to be there to make sure there are no more screw-ups. You have until Saturday." Ethan hung up before Carl could respond.

He was so tired of dealing with inept people. He should've gone after Jenna himself or at the very least gotten her to sign over the deed to the land before she ran. The garage that sat on the property was useless without it.

Stupid bitch!

She should know better than to try to strong arm him. He'd just have to consult his attorney to see if there were any charges he could level against Jenna for hindering the business transaction.

Every day she was out there running around the countryside cost Ethan thousands of dollars. Thanks to her, he was hemorrhaging money.

He should've known that someone with Jenna's spotty background would only cause him trouble. Ethan hoped his family never found out that he'd slept with the whore.

* * * * *

Jenna's first day on the job at the Gazette had been frankly boring compared to the unconventional introduction she'd received yesterday.

Paul had spent the morning badgering her about the interview with Aidan. He'd only stopped once she'd agreed to try her best, but Jenna had made it clear that her acceptance wasn't a promise of success.

Half the time the phone stopped ringing before Molly answered it. For a receptionist, she didn't seem overly concerned about the missed phone calls.

Instead, Molly continued her barrage of questions about Aidan. By noon, she had finally stopped calling him a vampire—thanks in large part to Jenna's assurance that she'd seen him in sunlight.

After being worn down all morning, Jenna had agreed to go to lunch with her.

Molly turned out to be a font of information. Jenna now knew that Ted was dating Alex. Though she hadn't met either one yet. And that Carol had finally 'come out' to her family, which as it turns out wasn't a surprise to anyone.

Thanks to the little gossip, Jenna also found out a lot about Paul Welling. According to Molly, he used to be a big city reporter. He'd fallen on hard times once it was discovered that he'd fabricated a couple of major stories. His previous employer had been sued and Paul had been let go. He'd been trying to carve his way back ever since.

That didn't bode well for Aidan. Paul's shady past coupled with his need to regain his reputation could lead him to do just about anything, print anything.

Five o'clock arrived after what felt like an eternity. Jenna rolled her neck to ease the stiffness and scanned the road behind her. Nothing. Forty-five minutes later, she spotted the entrance to the driveway and made a right.

The estate gate opened the second she buzzed to announce that she'd returned. Thanks to her co-workers fanciful stories, Jenna found herself scanning the woods for wolves. She'd seen one yesterday, but one hardly accounted for the rumors.

A couple of times Jenna thought she caught a flash of movement amongst the trees, but whatever it was disappeared too quickly to be positively identified.

The trees parted and the estate appeared. A mix of old world charm and modern architecture, the design fit its owner. Her heart raced as she scanned the yard. Was she really hoping to catch another glimpse of Aidan Fortier?

If Jenna were being honest with herself, then the answer would be yes. There was something about him that drew her to him. Sure, he was gorgeous and rolling in money, but that wasn't what fascinated her. Aidan was a puzzle.

Jenna had never been able to resist puzzles. She loved twisting the pieces to see how they fit together. It was one of the reasons she'd become a mechanic. Engines were like giant landscape jigsaws. They only worked when they were assembled in the right order.

Aidan had only presented her with a few pieces. Not nearly enough to form a clear picture of him. The stories she'd heard at the paper only added to his mystique and made her itch to know more.

"Like you need that kind of trouble," she muttered to herself.

Paul's thinly veiled warning rang in her ears. *Get the job done or get out.*

What choice did she have?

The driveway forked near the house. Jenna veered left and continued on another hundred yards. She pulled up in front of what she hoped was the garage. Several vehicles were parked haphazardly in the gravel lot.

Jenna tucked the Rover into a space and cut the engine. She jumped out, not bothering to lock it. Pebbles crunched under her feet as she walked to the door on the side of the building.

She heard men laughing inside and the sound of tools hitting metal. The combo drowned out the soft music playing in the background. Jenna poked her head inside. Her presence killed the conversation.

"Who are you?" one of the men asked, stepping away from a Lincoln MKX. "And what are you doing here unescorted?"

Unescorted? What did he mean by that? "I'm Jenna." She gestured to the Bug. "I just wanted to make sure my car made it here." She loved her car and was determined to get it running again. "Aidan said it would be okay to work on it."

The man glanced at her car and scratched his head. "Not sure when we're going to have time to get to it. We have our hands full right now." He jerked his chin toward to the Lincoln and the truck on racks beside it.

Jenna bit back a smile. He wasn't the first man to assume that she needed help. He wouldn't be the last. "That's all right. I think I can handle it on my own."

The man's gaze turned more assessing.

"Don't worry, I won't get in the way." The smell of grease and sweat greeted Jenna as she entered the garage, reminding her of home.

The large space had several bays, but only three were used for repair. The rest held luxury sedans and sports cars. Each work bay came equipped with hydraulic lifts and enough diagnostic equipment to open a shop.

Various sized tires were stacked against the right wall. Shelving units containing standard parts lined the back. To the left of the tires, a row of tools hung above a long workbench, organized from small to large and by type.

The man who'd questioned her stepped forward and gave

her a sheepish grin, which was at odds with his hulking size. "I'm Nic. That's Bernie." He hiked his thumb over his shoulder to point to the man under the hood of the Lincoln. "And that's Josh." The latter stood near the rear of the car and didn't look old enough to drive. He smiled and waved as their eyes met.

"Nice to meet you," Jenna said. "I'll let you get back to it."

Nic continued to stare at her.

"I'll call you, if I need you," she said.

"Sure." Nic hesitated, then backed into a tray of tools. The tray crashed onto the ground, sending socket wrenches and screwdrivers skittering across the concrete floor.

"Might help if you look where you're going," Bernie said.

Jenna watched crimson creep into Nic's cheeks.

He spun around, took one step, and tripped over a crowbar. Nic grunted and somehow kept his feet under him. That didn't stop Bernie and Josh from busting a gut though.

"Something got you distracted, Nic?" Josh howled with laughter.

"Keep it up, pup," Nic muttered.

Jenna poked her head under the Bug's bonnet, so Nic wouldn't see her laughing, but she couldn't stop her shoulders from shaking.

The laughter gradually faded and the men went back to work.

Jenna grabbed a nearby light and clipped it to the metal frame, then slowly examined the engine. While she did, she couldn't help but overhear the conversation taking place beside her.

"I changed out the right rear hub bearing assembly," Nic said. "That got rid of the noise, but caused a glitch in the ABS braking system. Now I have speed sensor code being set during the test drive."

In her peripheral, she saw Josh glance her way, then

quickly turn his attention back to the job. "I can't figure out why you're getting an ABS light and no speed signal from the wheel with the new hub bearing assembly in place."

They bantered various theories and suggestions back and forth, but no one was coming up with a solution. Jenna stopped what she was doing. "It's none of my business," she said, "but did you happen to use an aftermarket assembly?"

Three sets of eyes locked onto her. Nic hitched his hip against the side of the car. "Let's say that I did."

"Then that's your problem," Jenna said. "You need to use the Ford OEM assembly. The aftermarket assembly's toner ring doesn't play nice with the Ford sensor."

"How many days have you been working on the problem, Nic?" Bernie asked. "Three? Four?" He laughed. "Jenna here just fixed it in five minutes."

Nic flushed.

"Don't bust his chops too bad," Jenna said. "The only reason I knew what the problem was, is because I went through the same issue at my...at the," she corrected, "garage I worked at a few months back. Course it only took me two days to figure it out." She winked at Bernie.

The men roared with laughter. Jenna joined in, feeling relaxed and at home for the first time in months. She missed this kind of camaraderie. It seemed like a lifetime ago that she'd stepped foot inside a garage.

Until now, she hadn't dared. It would've been the first place Ethan and Carl Rich would've looked for her, the first place they would've checked.

"See, that proves you're a better mechanic than old Nic here." Josh playfully dug his elbow into Nic's ribs.

"He would've figured it out eventually...once he stopped staring at my butt," she said.

"Busted!" Josh shouted.

Jenna grinned at him, then went back to work on her car.

* * * * *

CHAPTER SIX

Aidan tried to keep his distance, but he couldn't ignore Jenna's sweet scent floating on the breeze. The alluring aroma wrapped around his senses, leaving him dizzy.

He'd intended to work, instead he found himself following his nose all the way to the garage. As he passed the Rover, he spotted Jenna's bag in the back.

Why hadn't she dropped it off at her motel last night? He shrugged it off and continued to the door.

Aidan stepped inside. A wrench hit the concrete with a loud clang. All three men slipped out from beneath the hood of the car to face him. Jenna didn't notice that he was there, until Nic muted the music.

She popped her head up. "Hey, that was my favorite song."

Aidan moved into her personal space and cleared his throat. Jenna spun around, pressing a hand to her chest. Her eyes widened, when she saw him. Was it his imagination or had her pupils dilated?

"Aidan," she croaked. "What are you doing here?"

He did his best to ignore the men's gaping mouths. "I thought I'd check to see that you had everything that you need."

"Uh. That's kind of you. Thanks!" Jenna took a step back and focused on her car.

She probably thought he wouldn't see her blush.

"I believe I have everything I need," she said.

"Good. How is the Rover working out?" Aidan rolled his shoulders. He didn't like having an audience, especially when the conversation was so awkward. He'd never had trouble speaking to women, not even when he was a pup. Being tongue-tied was a new experience for him. One Aidan didn't like one bit.

Jenna rubbed her face, smearing grease across her cheek. "It's great. Thanks again for letting me use the space."

"Sir," Nic interrupted. "Did you need something?"

Aidan's attention remained on Jenna. He didn't bother to glance at Nic. "No."

"It's just that you never come down here," Nic said.

Aidan's wolf brushed his skin as he slowly turned to face his mechanic. "Then it's high time that I did."

Nic's blue eyes glowed.

Aidan bristled.

Nic's gaze immediately dropped to the floor. "Of course. Let us know if you want to see anything in particular." He glanced at Jenna, which only made Aidan's hackles rise even more. The tension in the space increased.

"I will." He showed more teeth than was necessary. Aidan didn't like the wolf's interest in Jenna, but he let it go...for now.

It shouldn't matter to him if Nic and Jenna went out. If anything, he should try to encourage the relationship. It would take her off his hands and hopefully get her out of his thoughts.

His wolf snarled in protest.

Before Aidan could examine his wolf's odd response, Robert LaBeouf popped his head into the garage.

"Sir, you have a phone call," he said.

Aidan sighed. The work of an Alpha never ended. He rubbed the back of his neck. Aidan wasn't ready to leave yet. He hadn't gotten his fill of Jenna's lilac scent.

"I'll be there in a moment," he said.

Robert hesitated like he was about to say more, but caught Aidan's censorious glare. "I'll let them know."

"You do that."

"Your garage is incredible." Jenna's comment drew his mind away from the unwanted distractions. "Better than..." She stopped short. "I should get back to work. It was nice seeing you again."

Aidan nodded, feeling oddly disappointed as he left the garage. She'd dismissed him. Dismissed him like he was some kind of annoying pup, nipping at her heels. Aidan had never been dismissed before. Not by a woman. He had no experience with this type of rejection and wasn't altogether certain how he should act.

Bernie followed him out. "Alpha, can I have a word?"

"Can it wait?" Aidan needed to get away from the garage. Away from *her*.

Bernie glanced toward the open door, then lowered his voice. "No, it's about Jenna."

Aidan halted immediately. "What about her?"

Bernie's nervous gaze darted to the garage once more.

"She's human," Aidan said. "She's not going to be able to hear us."

His shoulders slumped in relief. "I think she's been living in her car," Bernie said.

Shocked by the statement, Aidan moved them away from the entrance. "Why would you think that?" His chest clenched at the thought of Jenna being in such a vulnerable position.

"I don't have proof," Bernie said. "But her scent is unusually strong in the Bug's backseat. And I found a tremendous amount of food packaging material scattered throughout the car."

"Are you sure she's not a slob?" Aidan asked. It wasn't unusual for humans to use their cars for trash heaps.

Bernie shook his head. "Don't think so. I also found a blanket rolled up and tucked into a side panel. Taken individually, I wouldn't think much of it, but when you add in her scent..." Bernie tapped his nose. "I just thought you should know."

Aidan nodded his thanks, then walked over to the Rover and opened the back door. He leaned in and inhaled deeply.

Jenna's scent filled his lungs. Aidan breathed in again and frowned. "You're right. Her scent is all over the backseat. There's only one reason for that. She must've slept in here last night. But why?"

Bernie shrugged. "The stuff I found in the Bug was old—at least a couple of weeks. I wouldn't be surprised if some of it is even older."

Had she been living in her car for months?

Aidan stared at the backseat. It didn't make sense. Why was Jenna living out of her car? She obviously had skills. Without them, she wouldn't have a job at the paper or be able to repair her car.

Bernie stepped toward the garage and stopped. "I've got an extra room in town—"

"No!" The vehemence in Aidan's response shocked them both. "I mean that's not necessary."

"She can't stay in the SUV," he said.

"She won't be," Aidan said.

Bernie's brow furrowed. "I've only known her for a couple of hours, but I can tell you right now that the girl is proud. No way is she going to let us help her, if she thinks we're trying to give her a handout."

"Leave it to me." Aidan's mind raced, but kept coming back to only one option. It was sheer insanity on his part, but what choice did he have? He couldn't let Jenna sleep in the vehicle. It wasn't safe. For some reason Aidan *needed* her to be safe.

He glanced at the sky. The moon peeked out from behind the tops of the trees. Not quite full yet, but it would be soon. When that happened, the estate would transform. He would transform.

It will only be for a couple of days. She'll be gone long before the moon run, he told himself.

Aidan stared at her bag in the back of the Rover. What kind of Alpha would he be, if he let her leave without at least trying to convince her to stay?

The phone call could wait. If it were important, they'd call back. Aidan shut the Rover's door and walked back into the garage. Jenna was once again under the hood of her car. "I was thinking," he said.

She gasped. Her head shot up and hit the hood. "Ouch! Stop sneaking up on me."

"Sorry." Aidan fought the urge to walk over and examine her. Touching her was a bad idea, especially when he needed to convince her to stay. "You okay?"

Jenna rubbed her head. "I'll be fine. What were you saying?"

"I was thinking about the repairs you need to do on your car," he said, not entirely sure where he was going with this idea.

She paled. "What about them?"

"It's ridiculous that you aren't able to work on the vehicle anytime you like," he said.

Confusion marred her face. "I can't. I have a job."

"I know." His nose wrinkled in disgust. "That's not what I meant. I thought it might be easier for you, if you stayed here at the estate—at least while you're working on the car. That way you could do the repairs anytime you felt like it. You wouldn't have to worry about driving back to your motel every night."

The last of the blood in her face drained away and her scent soured. It was as Bernie suspected.

Aidan pretended not to notice her reaction. What if she

turned down his offer? What would he do then? He couldn't order her to stay. Jenna wasn't part of his pack. He couldn't hold her against her will. Though that thought held some appeal.

His wolf perked up. *Forget about it. Not going to happen.* Aidan's heart pounded. The need to protect thrummed in his head, as he waited for her answer.

* * * * *

Everything inside of Jenna screamed for her to say no, but Aidan was right. If she were here, she could spend every moment of extra time that she had working on her car. It would be a relief to not worry about driving back to the campground every night.

Staying on the estate would also give her the opportunity to interview Aidan. Jenna liked the idea of getting to know the real man behind the success, solving the puzzle that was Aidan Fortier.

Jenna bit her lip. "I don't want to put you out." Pride reared its ugly head.

"You won't," Aidan said. "As you've seen, the house is quite large. There's plenty of room for one more."

"If you're sure?" Say yes! Her brain screamed. She'd never get a better chance than this.

"I am." Aidan cleared his throat. "Now if you'll excuse me. I've kept whoever is on the phone waiting long enough."

"They've probably already hung up," she said.

Aidan smiled. "That's highly unlikely. When you're finished here, find Robert. He'll have a room waiting."

"Thank you," Jenna said.

Their eyes met fleetingly, long enough for Jenna to see the heat burning behind Aidan's amber gaze. In a blink it was gone, but there was no doubt in her mind that it had been there. Most shocking of all was her reaction to it. To him.

With one look, Aidan made her want. Made her ache. Her body had been dormant for three months. Now suddenly it was awake, aware of what it had been missing. And Jenna wasn't sure how to handle that.

When in doubt—run!

Jenna opened her mouth to tell Aidan that she'd changed her mind.

"Please excuse me, I really must go," he interjected, before she got the chance.

She glanced over her shoulder. All three mechanics busied themselves, pretending that they hadn't been listening to every word.

Bernie looked at her.

"What?" she asked.

"Nothing." He grinned, then grabbed the remote from Nic and turned up the music.

* * * * *

Aidan spent twenty tedious minutes on the phone, listening to all the areas that the southern Moonlight Kin pack Alpha would like to see reformed.

Some of his ideas were genuinely innovative, while others simply rehashed old notions and outdated concepts. Aidan tried to concentrate on what Pierre was saying, but his thoughts refused to leave Jenna.

He didn't like the idea of her out there in the garage surrounded by his wolves. She was perfectly safe, but Nic had shown far too much interest in her for his peace of mind.

Now that she was under his roof, Aidan felt responsible for her. It was his duty to protect her, especially from his wolves.

Pierre said something else that Aidan missed. This was ridiculous. They were going to have to have this whole conversation over again, but not tonight.

"Rest assured that I will bring up your suggestions at the

next Lycanian Elder meeting." He gave the southern Alpha his standard political reply and excused himself.

The second he hung up, Aidan pressed a buzzer to summon Robert into his office. His assistant entered, his face drawn in concern.

"Sir, I noticed that Ms. Dane is still here," he said. "Should I tell her that it's time to head back to town? I can't help but think she's taking advantage of your hospitality."

No one took advantage of him. Aidan wouldn't allow it. "Jenna will be staying with us for a few days," he said. "I'd intended to let you know before I answered the phone, but I'd kept Pierre waiting long enough."

"Jenna?" Robert startled. "But Alpha, the wolves were planning to run tonight."

Aidan played with the miniature Zen garden on his desk, but the repetitive sand raking did little to bring him inner peace. "Make sure that they shift in the woods and tell them to keep away from the house."

"But Alpha, we risk exposure with her here," he said.

Aidan set the tiny rake down. He was well aware of the risks. He didn't need reminding. Perhaps he should be more concerned about Jenna given the phase of the moon, but she'd already faced down one wolf without batting an eyelash. He didn't think she'd wilt, if she accidentally caught sight of a few more.

"My orders are clear," he said. "Prepare a room for her in the west wing."

Robert shifted in place. "Wouldn't she be more comfortable in the east wing?"

"With the pack?" Aidan arched a brow. "Do you think that would be wise?"

Robert shook his head. "I was merely concerned for your safety. Humans are untrustworthy vermin. If it were up to me, I'd send her away or have her exterminated, before she has a chance to 'infect' the pack."

Aidan rose from behind his desk. "Of that I have no

doubt, but since you are not in a position to give orders..."

It was rare that he had to remind any of his people of their position in the pack, but today Aidan found himself doing so twice.

It was his fault. He'd given Robert far too much leeway, too much responsibility in hopes that he'd slip up and reveal where his true loyalties lie. He hadn't yet. But the small shift in power had gone to his head and made Robert forget his place.

Robert paled. "If that is all, I'll notify the maids to prepare her room."

Aidan nodded. "You do that."

He stopped at the door, pausing with his hand on the knob. Color had returned to his face, but Robert couldn't meet Aidan's gaze. "Do you still want me to send another female to your room tonight? Or would you rather *rest*?"

Aidan ground his teeth. The gossip from his encounter with Sydney had obviously reached his assistant's attentive ears. Robert's gleeful expression only made matters worse.

Last night was an anomaly. Tonight he'd prove it. "I have no need to rest, when duty calls."

Robert coughed. "Nine o'clock okay?"

"That would be perfect." His wolf grumbled. Aidan ignored it. Just because Jenna Dane was staying at the estate didn't mean that anything in his life had to change.

* * * * *

Jenna settled into the bedroom that Aidan had selected for her. Soft cream colors and earth-tone browns served to decorate the cozy room. A small dresser sat against one wall, while a queen-sized bed smothered in pillows graced another, leaving Jenna spoiled for choice.

How long had it been since she'd slept in this kind of bed? Three months? Longer? She'd certainly never owned anything this nice. Jenna had poured every penny she earned back into her business.

The bedroom had an ensuite bath attached that came fully stocked with shampoo, soap, and several fluffy towels. She stared at the bathtub longingly. Jenna couldn't wait to take a long soak.

She leaned down to turn on the water, but was interrupted by a knock at the door. Jenna gave the tub a longing glance, then crossed the room to open the door.

Robert LaBeouf stood in the hall with a tray of food in his hands. He didn't wait for her to invite him inside. He simply stepped by her and placed the tray on a small table situated by the sliding glass doors.

"I wasn't sure what people like you normally eat, so I had the chef put a little bit of everything on the tray. It should keep you until morning. There should be no need to leave the room."

His tone was perfectly polite, but his words and demeanor gave Jenna pause. Robert made it sound like she was a prisoner, not a guest. Was Molly wrong about this being a cult?

Aidan didn't strike her as the type to pass around the Kool-Aid, but he was certainly charismatic enough to garner a lot of followers. She made a mental note to check the door to make sure it couldn't be locked from the outside.

Jenna didn't know why Robert didn't like her, since they'd had very little interaction. Maybe protecting his boss was part of his job description?

Made sense. Aidan's wealth automatically made him a target.

Or maybe Robert had a distrustful nature? Of course, there was always a possibility that he was just a dick. For some people that state of being came naturally.

Aidan didn't strike her as the type of man who needed defending, but Jenna couldn't say for sure, since she really didn't know him.

"Please tell Aidan thank you again for the use of the

room." She hoped her gratitude would smooth Robert's ruffled feathers. If anything, it made matters worse.

Robert stiffened at the familiar use of Aidan's name. "*Mr. Fortier* is *occupied* this evening." He paused, letting the words and their meaning sink in. "I'll be sure to tell him in the *morning* that you find the room adequate."

Jenna waited for Aidan's stuffy assistant to leave, then checked the door. To her relief, the only lock was on the inside.

Once she was convinced that Robert couldn't trap her, she sat down to eat. The food should've been delicious, but instead, it dropped like boulders into her stomach.

Who cares what—or *who* Aidan was doing tonight? Certainly not her. Their relationship was purely professional. And it needed to stay that way so she could remain impartial during the interview.

Jenna snorted. Fat chance of that after everything he'd done for her.

Besides, Aidan hadn't agreed to an interview yet. If his history was anything to go by, he would likely decline her offer.

Jenna put her fork down and pushed the tray aside. She needed air, but didn't feel like facing Robert's misplaced scorn. Her gaze strayed to the sliding glass doors. Jenna pulled the curtains aside and glanced out. The stone patio appeared to be vacant.

Perfect.

The lock opened with a soft click and she stepped out into the temperate air. Jenna wrapped her arms around herself and took a deep breath, feeling some of the tension leave her body. The aroma of freshly mowed lawn greeted her, but it was the movement in the woods that surrounded the yard that captured her attention.

Red eyes glowed in the darkness like demonic fireflies amongst the trees. Jenna caught a glimpse of fur and saw a bushy tail swish.

Wolves!

And not just one from the looks of it. A whole pack.

The stories from town came rushing back. "Every story holds an element of truth," she murmured.

Just because the man had wolves on his property didn't mean he was a werewolf or a vampire.

The wolves nudged each other with their massive heads, yipping playfully as they darted amongst the tree trunks. If they noticed her, they didn't care. They were obviously used to seeing humans.

Jenna's dour mood lifted as she watched them scamper about. What would it be like to belong to such a tightknit family?

She couldn't even imagine. She'd spent her life moving trash bags full of clothes from one foster house to the next, doing her best to avoid getting too attached, while dodging the occasional molester. That had been her life, her only world, until she'd aged out of the system.

The process had taught Jenna that she couldn't count on anyone but herself. There was no such thing as the perfect family. It was an illusion, a fairytale, a dream she'd stopped believing in a long time ago.

Better to live vicariously through animals than to delude herself. At least their instincts were honest.

Jenna watched the wolves interact, marveling at their closeness. If only people could learn to work together for the good of the 'pack', the world would be a much better place.

* * * * *

CHAPTER SEVEN

Tonight was the night. Aidan stood in his room, wearing nothing but a pair of low-slung black jeans. His feet were bare as he paced across the carpet, nerves on edge.

Even though Jenna's room was on the floor beneath his, Aidan kept thinking that he could *hear* her. It was his imagination. The walls and floors in his home had been soundproofed for Were privacy. What he hadn't imagined was the sweet aroma of lilacs wafting on the air. The scent followed him wherever he went.

He heard shuffling in the hall outside his door. What if Jenna was lost and needed his help? Without thought, Aidan crossed the room and opened the door before anyone could knock.

Lisa's arm hovered in the air. Her gray eyes widened in surprise. She lowered her hand and took a step back.

"You called for me, Alpha?"

"Yes, come in." Aidan concealed his disappointment, ignoring the *wrongness* in his gut.

The sooner they got this over with, the sooner he could prove to himself and the pack that everything was normal. *He was normal.* The presence of one human female wasn't going to stop him from performing his duties.

"It's been a long day, so if you don't mind I'd like to get started." Aidan wanted to find his bondmate and put an end to the tryouts.

Lisa flushed, but stepped inside the room and shut the door behind her. "As you wish, Alpha." She quickly stripped off her clothes, revealing her womanly body. "Where do you want me?" There was huskiness to her voice that hadn't been there before.

Aidan pointed to the bed, then his hand moved to the buttons on his jeans. He shucked his clothes quickly.

Lisa licked her lips as her gaze traveled down the length of his naked body.

Aidan had never seen the need for modesty. Like all wolves, running through the woods kept him in shape. He was proud of his form, happy that it pleased both Were and human females, though he'd never acted upon any attraction with a human.

The memory of Jenna's dilated pupils popped into his mind. He hadn't imagined the heat simmering between them. Her scent had warmed, grown richer, deeper, when she'd looked at him.

What would it be like to hold her in his arms? Sink into her body? Have her writhing beneath him? His shaft hardened at the thought.

"Alpha?"

Aidan blinked and the room came back into focus. Instead of Jenna, Lisa lay on his bed, her firm thighs slightly parted, giving him a tantalizing glimpse of the moisture gathering in her soft folds.

The sight should've enhanced his erection, instead his shaft wilted like an over-watered plant.

She pursed her lips. "I want to touch you."

Touching was good. Touching would help bring his mind and body back into alignment. Aidan mentally smacked his wolf upside the head to get its attention.

Once he had it, Aidan nodded to Lisa to proceed. He could do this. Last night was a fluke. His hands clenched at his sides as he kneeled on the foot of the bed to give her better access.

"Wait," he said, before Lisa could grasp him. Aidan leaned over and dug his nose into the soft curls between her legs.

She mewed and her eyes drifted shut. "Yes!" she hissed.

Her deliciously musky scent filled his lungs. He could do this. It was just like riding a bike.

Aidan's wolf snorted.

"Touch me," he said, ignoring it. He was in control, not his beast.

Lisa grasped his shaft and stroked him, trying to bring it back to life. The normally dependable part of his anatomy once again refused to rise.

His inner wolf snickered. It had won this battle, but the war for control of his body wasn't over.

Aidan pulled away and slid off the bed, hoping Lisa hadn't noticed. He scrubbed his hands over his face and through his hair. "I'm sorry, but you are not the one," he said.

Lisa's lower lip poked out. "But we haven't tried yet." Panic seeped into her voice.

"I don't need to. I can tell by your scent that you're not my bondmate," Aidan said.

Her brow furrowed. "I thought you needed to be inside me to be sure."

He did and he didn't. Aidan shook his head. In this instance, he just knew.

Lisa spread her legs wider. "Maybe you didn't get a good whiff. Why don't you try one more time?"

"I beg your pardon?" Aidan's brow shot to his hairline. How could she question his scenting abilities? "My nose is *not* broken."

She glanced at his flaccid shaft and mirrored his

expression. The implication clear.

Heat infused his face. Aidan snatched his denims off the floor and jerked them on without looking at her. "Leave!"

Her scent sharpened as anger replaced need. Lisa threw on her clothes and stomped to the door. "Sydney was right about your impotence," she muttered under her breath, just loud enough for him to hear.

"Get out!" Aidan bellowed.

Lisa slammed the door behind her.

Aidan rolled his shoulders, but it did little to alleviate the tension and fear building inside of him. He wasn't impotent. How could he be? He was a werewolf. His hand trembled as he scrubbed it over his chest.

Lisa's sour scent lingered in the air, choking him. Aidan couldn't breathe. He needed to get out of his bedroom, out of this house before the walls closed in and crushed him. He walked over to his French doors and threw them open.

The evening air smacked his face, clearing his lungs of the female Were's scent. Aidan walked to the balcony wall and leaned over it, hanging his head between his arms. He took several deep breaths.

What was he going to do? He couldn't go on like this? It had only been two days, but soon news of his 'affliction' would reach the ears of the Lycanian Elders, then there would be questions. Questions he couldn't—wouldn't answer. If this continued, he'd have no choice but to step down as Alpha. The pack needed a mated leader.

He inhaled once again, filling his lungs. This time he caught Jenna's floral aroma. He heard the tread of a shoe scraping against stone. Aidan's ears perked. He leaned over the balcony, balancing on his stomach, and spotted Jenna standing on the patio below.

She didn't notice him, didn't hear him. Her gaze remained trained on the trees. Aidan followed her line of sight and saw his wolves moving beneath the branches.

He cursed under his breath and strode back into his

bedroom. Three minutes later, Aidan found himself dressed and standing at the foot of the stairs that led to the lower patio.

Aidan watched Jenna from the shadows, unable to look away. Her hair glowed like fairy-fire in the burgeoning moonlight, giving her an ethereal appearance.

She'd make a beautiful wolf. The thought came unbidden into his mind, leaving him shaken. As tempting as it was, biting her would be sheer madness.

He might be temporarily 'afflicted', but Aidan wasn't insane enough to act upon the impulse. His gaze drifted over her.

Jenna wore a pair of black leggings that clung to her like a thin layer of paint, cupping her lush bottom. An over-sized sweater and T-shirt concealed her firm high breasts, but Aidan knew they were there.

She leaned over the wall, her head dropping down to look at something on the ground. The move lifted her ass, making her appear submissive.

Aidan's wolf shoved him aside to get a better look. When he tried to push the beast back down, it snapped and growled at him. Aidan couldn't tear his gaze away from her. He wanted. He needed. His mouth watered as blood from his brain rushed south.

It wasn't until the buttons on his denims bit into his shaft that Aidan noticed how hard he'd become. He glanced down in disbelief at the bulge filling the front of his denims.

You picked a fine time to start working again. He stared at his erection in bewilderment.

His wolf barked inside his head to get his attention, then urged him to act.

Not going to happen, Aidan spoke directly to his beast. *You're only interested in her because she's human. That makes her unique to you. To us. That's the only reason you want her. It's also the reason you can't have her.*

The wolves in the woods sensed his presence and howled.

Jenna didn't even flinch at the sound. Instead, she leaned even further over the short wall. She was killing him. Aidan closed his eyes and prayed for strength.

"I wouldn't do that if I were you." He adjusted himself, then stepped out of the darkness.

Jenna nearly toppled before catching herself. "You really have to stop sneaking up on me."

"I wasn't sneaking. You were too preoccupied with the wolves to hear me."

She glanced back at the trees and scowled. "I think you scared them away."

Doubtful, Aidan thought.

"Aren't you afraid?" he asked.

She edged away from him as he drew nearer. "Of what?"

Of me? Of the beast you sense lurking inside of me?

"The savage beasts in the woods." He motioned to where the wolves had been milling only moments ago.

Jenna stopped her retreat and her green eyes narrowed.

Aidan's lips canted at her sudden mood change. She had a lot of courage for a human. He'd give her that.

"They're not beasts." She chided. "Not in the sense that you mean. And they're certainly not savage, unless they're starving. As someone who keeps wolves on his property, I would think you'd know the difference."

Jenna was scolding him, actually scolding him. No one scolded him. So why did that make him so damned pleased?

"I didn't mean to offend you." Aidan planted his hip against the wall. "It's just that a lot of people don't see wolves that way. They look at them as pests, nuisances in need of extermination. Instead of an apex species that keeps the animal population healthy and in balance."

She looked at him. "If humans had half the sense of family that wolves do, then there wouldn't be so many abused and neglected kids in the world."

"Are you speaking from experience?" The idea enraged him, but there was no denying the shadow of pain in her eyes.

Aidan tried to imagine what it would be like to have had his family reject him. He couldn't fathom it, the concept far too alien in the Lycan world.

"People take family for granted." Jenna's voice cracked as she dodged his question. "I don't."

What had happened to her? Was that why she was living in her car? She was too old to have runaway from foster care, but that didn't mean she hadn't grown up in the system. He clamped down on his anger. If he didn't, Aidan would end up shifting in front of her.

"What are you doing up?" He moved the conversation to a less volatile topic.

"Couldn't sleep. Thought maybe some fresh air would help, then I noticed the wolves and I guess I lost track of time. I didn't disturb your evening, did I?"

He shook his head. "No." At least not directly.

"Are you sure?" she asked.

Aidan crossed his arms over his chest and narrowed his eyes. "Why do you ask?"

Jenna's fingers curled around the top of the stone wall. "Your P.A. implied that you'd be occupied for the rest of the night and you were not to be disturbed."

What in Freki's teats had Robert told her?

"My plans changed," Aidan said.

Her gaze flicked to his, then skittered away. "Sorry." Her words didn't match the pleasing scent emanating from her skin. Was he the cause of it? For some reason, Aidan wanted to know.

"Don't be." He moved closer.

Her floral scent changed, became richer, muskier. With infinite care, he pushed a stray curl away from her face. Jenna's heart pounded so hard that he could hear it. His gaze flicked to the pulse jumping in her neck.

"So soft," he said.

"Thanks." She brushed a hand through her hair and

cleared her throat. "Is this some kind of animal sanctuary?"

The question brought him up short. Aidan had never thought about his estate in those exact terms, but the idea was close enough. "Something like that."

Jenna tilted her head. "You know people in town talk about your wolves."

His heart slammed against his ribs, but Aidan managed to maintain his calm exterior. "What exactly do they say?" He touched her hair again, the silky strands slipping through his fingers.

Jenna gave him an odd look, but she didn't pull away. "Honestly, I don't know where to start. They are a crazy bunch." She shook her head. "And when I say crazy, I mean *crazy*. They think you howl at the moon with your wolves like some kind of werewolf." She giggled, missing Aidan's startled expression.

"That's quite a theory," he said softly. "Wonder how they came by it?"

"You haven't heard the best one yet," she said.

"Can hardly wait," he deadpanned.

Her grin widened. "One person in town is convinced that you're a vampire." Jenna roared with laughter. "A vampire! Can you believe it?"

Aidan snorted. "As if I'd ever stoop to *that* level."

* * * * *

He was quiet for quite some time, then asked, "What do you think?"

Her gaze drifted to his sensual mouth. No fangs there. Were his lips as soft as they appeared to be? The urge to close the distance between them and find out nearly overwhelmed her.

Jenna shoved her hands in her pockets and tore her gaze away from his mouth. "It's true that you allow wolves to run loose on your property, but I haven't seen you howling at the

65

moon." She winked.

She was actually flirting with him. Jenna hadn't flirted with anyone in months. It felt good. Felt right. Even if it was a little awkward.

"It's not full yet," Aidan said dryly.

She laughed. "Right. I forgot." Jenna glanced at the moon, basking in its soft glow. Her smile faded. "I think people start rumors to make themselves feel better, feel superior to others. They don't know you, which makes them even more jealous of your success." Her gaze strayed to the house.

Aidan sighed. "Material things do not define who I am. You should know that by now."

His words shamed her. Aidan had gone above and beyond to help a total stranger. But Jenna had allowed a handsome face to sway her before. The consequence of which had destroyed everything she'd worked for.

It pained her to admit, but other than striking good looks, Aidan didn't have much in common with Ethan. It wasn't fair of her to compare them.

Jenna had been comparing people to her ex for three months and all it had done was make her bitter. She was tired of being bitter. She was tired of the distrust. Jenna was tired period.

She needed that chapter of her life to be over, so that she could be open to new things. Perhaps the things right in front of her.

Aidan's sharp amber eyes glowed the longer he stared at her. A trick of the light no doubt. The intensity of his gaze made it hard to breathe. Hard to think.

She casually moved to the side to give herself some space. If Aidan noticed, he didn't say anything. He turned his attention toward the trees.

"Why are you really here?" he asked.

Ice encased Jenna, leaving her shivering inside. "What do you mean?"

"Why Breakbend? Of all the places to settle, why did you come here?" he asked.

Some of the tension left her body. "Like a lot of people, I needed the work."

Aidan glanced at her. "That doesn't explain why you're on the run."

She flinched. "Who said anything about...I don't know where you got that idea from, but you're mistaken."

"Am I?"

Jenna nodded, but couldn't meet his gaze.

"Do you know why I'm so successful in business?" he asked, throwing her off balance.

She shrugged stiffly. "Because you've developed innovative software?"

Aidan shook his head, sending his black hair into his face. "No, it's because I have an uncanny ability to read people. My competitors, my business associates, my enemies, and my friends. I know without fail, when someone is lying to me." He reached out and clasped her hand.

Fire shot up Jenna's arm, melting the ice as it spread throughout her body. She couldn't catch her breath.

Pull away, her mind screamed, but her hand refused to cooperate.

"You're not a liar," Aidan said, "but you're definitely hiding something."

Her stomach ricocheted off her knees, then bounced into her throat. "I'm tired," she said abruptly. "I think I'm going to head to bed. Thanks again for the room. I'll do my best to get the car fixed tomorrow, and then I will be on my way." She took a step toward her room, forgetting that he still held her hand.

The warmth of his fingers scalded her. Their gazes met and lingered. Aidan stepped closer and leaned in next to her ear. His warm breath brushed her skin, making her nipples harden.

"You're safe here, Jenna," he murmured. "I'm a good

friend to have." *And a worse enemy*, was left unspoken. "I offer you my protection freely. No strings attached." His lips brushed her jawbone.

Jenna closed her eyes and shuddered. Her resolve wavered. The urge to come clean burned her esophagus as the words tangled in her throat.

She wanted to trust him. Wanted to believe what he was saying was true, but she didn't know Aidan Fortier. And he certainly didn't know her.

Still, it was a tempting offer, but he didn't realize the trouble she was hauling in her wake. Aidan might genuinely mean what he'd said, but Jenna had been wrong before.

Jenna couldn't risk it—not even for him. She wouldn't survive another betrayal.

"Goodnight, Aidan." This time when Jenna stepped back, he released her.

His jaw tightened, but he didn't say another word. Aidan simply nodded, then turned back to face the woods.

* * * * *

Whatever she was running from had Jenna spooked. You didn't have to be a werewolf to see that. He'd only known her for two days, but Aidan needed her to trust him. He refused to look at why it was so important. Her scent faded, replaced by the thick green growth of the woods.

Something moved to his right. Aidan's hackles rose. He swiftly inhaled, scenting the night air. He caught a wisp of sweetness and expected to see a female Were.

Robert stepped from the shadows.

How long had he been standing there watching and listening? The fact that Aidan hadn't noticed him until now was testament to how much Jenna distracted him.

Aidan checked to make sure that Jenna's sliding door was closed. "You were supposed to order the wolves to stay in the woods." Without another word, he moved them to the far end of the porch.

"I relayed your message," Robert said. "But I cannot make them follow orders. Only the Alpha has that power."

Aidan bristled. "The Alpha is who gave them the order to stay away."

Robert looked down at the stone floor. "Did they scare the human?"

He sounded hopeful.

Aidan watched him closely. "Their appearance intrigued her. She wanted to get closer, to know more. Maybe even become part of the pack." The idea wasn't as appalling as it should be, but he'd said it to see how Robert reacted.

"We can't let in strays! She wasn't born Lycan. She's not one of us." Robert's eyes glowed with barely contained fury. "What did you tell her?"

Interesting...

"I didn't tell her anything," Aidan said. "She came up with her own conclusions."

Robert searched his face. "And what conclusions would those be?" he asked.

"She believes the estate is a wildlife refuge." Aidan kept his expression bland and crossed his arms over his chest. "I saw no need to correct her assumption."

Robert sighed and deflated under scrutiny. "I suppose there are worse things for her to believe," he said. "It isn't safe for her to be here. For her or for the pack."

Aidan strode down the stairs into the backyard, leaving Robert scrambling to catch up. "I will handle Jenna Dane. There's no need for concern."

"I'm only looking out for the pack, Alpha."

"As am I!" He growled low in his throat. "The only reason I allow you to question my judgment is because of your loyalty to the pack. Do not make me regret my decision."

Aidan was under no illusion, when it came to Robert's loyalty to him. Because of his lack of strength, Robert would suck up to any Alpha—or potential Alpha in order to maintain his current position. Without his job, Robert would drop to the bottom of the pack.

"Yes, Alpha." Robert's gaze burned holes in the grass, but he never looked up.

Aidan stripped his clothes off. "I'm going to go for a run." He walked to the edge of the woods and glanced at Jenna's darkened room. Aidan saw the curtains part, then he felt her heated gaze upon his bare skin.

She might not trust him, but she did *want* him. That was a start.

Aidan stood in plain view for longer than he normally would have. He wanted Jenna to see him. Wanted her to want him as much as his wolf wanted her.

It shouldn't want her at all, something inside him snapped.

Aidan waited a few seconds more, then stepped behind a tree. Black fur rippled over his skin and claws sprang from his fingertips as he shifted, freeing his Other form. Aidan threw his head back and howled, then took off in search of the rest of the pack.

** * * * **

Jenna was convinced that she'd swallowed her tongue. That was the only reason for the strangled gasp that had come from her throat, when she watched Aidan strip off his clothes and walk toward the woods.

She couldn't hear what he was saying. There'd been no reason that she could see for him to stop walking, but he had. And for that, Jenna would be eternally grateful.

Never in all her years of existence had she ever seen anything more shocking or more spectacular. The man was gorgeous from his head to his...oh my.

Her body clenched.

That particular part of his anatomy had to be a trick of the light. Jenna gulped and tried not to drool.

Too bad he was crazy as a loon. Because only a crazy person would walk into woods, teaming with wild wolves. Naked as the day he was born.

Jenna watched until he'd disappeared, then slipped into bed. She closed her eyes, doing her very best to erase Aidan's naked body from her mind. But no matter how long she laid there, Jenna couldn't forget.

The more she thought about him, the more she ached. She turned over and punched the pillow.

His perfect male form haunted her, turning her thoughts carnal, before she drifted to sleep.

* * * * *

CHAPTER EIGHT

Long, strawberry blond curls brushed Aidan's abdomen, causing gooseflesh to rise over his skin. His stomach muscles contracted as moist lips brushed an open-mouthed kiss over his navel.

"Jenna," he hissed, sinking his fingers into her hair.

Her green eyes sparkled mischievously, as she moved his hands away and placed them on the bed beside him. She grinned and went right back to raining kisses over his chest.

Aidan fisted the sheets to keep from reaching for her again. His swollen shaft ached as her lips skirted around it, teasing him, tormenting him. She was trying to destroy him.

Her curls caressed his thighs and Aidan trembled. Jenna's blunt nails dug into his legs as she pushed them apart and positioned her body between them. She looked at him once more from beneath her long lashes. Their gazes locked and embers burst into flames.

Jenna lowered her head. Her lips drew closer and closer to the place he needed them most. Aidan's shaft bounced against his belly. He stared, transfixed by the sight of her and held his breath. Jenna's lips parted and she...*chirped.*

Aidan was too far gone to care. "Please don't stop," he

begged, his desperation dire.

Chirp! Chirp! Chirp!

Aidan frowned. What the hell? Why was she making that sound? Strike that—how was she making that sound?

Her breath brushed over him and he shuddered. Forget about the noise. Aidan wasn't going to let anything interrupt this moment. He was too close.

Chirp!

The sound was louder now. More insistent. Aidan squeezed his eyes closed, willing it to go away. When he opened them again, Jenna was gone.

"No!" He shot straight up in bed.

Sunlight poured into the room, temporarily blinding him. *Chirp! Chirp!* His gaze strayed to the alarm on the table.

Aidan closed his eyes and groaned. He hit the snooze button and fell back onto the bed, his body hot, hard, and trembling with need.

A dream.

It had all been a dream.

Disappointment hollowed his chest, leaving behind a soul-deep yearning he could no longer ignore.

* * * * *

Jenna didn't have to be into work until the afternoon, which was a good thing considering how fitfully she'd slept. Every time she'd tried to close her eyes, she'd seen Aidan's naked body. The image had been burned into her retinas.

In the moments she'd managed to catch some sleep, the dreams had taken over. Vivid, active, and so intense that they'd felt real. *He'd felt real.* She and Aidan had devoured each other, their bodies twining like boa constrictors in the middle of a mating frenzy.

Jenna threw back the covers and climbed out of bed. She might as well get some work done on the car, since there was no way she was going back to sleep. At this point, she didn't dare close her eyes.

She showered quickly, making good use of the adjustable massage head, then went to the garage. Her body still ached, despite the orgasm, but at least she'd taken some of the edge off. Jenna had had to do something, before she faced Aidan again.

The garage was empty when she arrived. It didn't take long to realize that her beloved Bug needed several new parts in order to run properly. Parts that weren't available in the garage. Parts that cost money. Money she didn't have. Wouldn't have, unless she could get an interview with Aidan.

She was still under the bonnet, where she'd been for an hour, when Nic and Bernie arrived. "Morning, guys." She peered beyond them. "Where's Josh?"

"He drove into the city last night to pick up more parts. Should be back later this afternoon," Bernie said.

Nic stared at her face and frowned. No doubt noticing the circles under her eyes. "You're up early," he said.

"Couldn't sleep. The wolves kept me up," she lied.

It hadn't been the wolves occupying her thoughts, but she wasn't about to tell them that she'd dreamt about their boss.

Both men froze and exchanged an odd glance. Bernie recovered first. "You should stay away from the monsters in the woods. They're dangerous. Every child familiar with Little Red Riding Hood knows that."

Was he kidding? Jenna couldn't tell, but something in his cautious expression told her that her response mattered. "The only monsters I've ever encountered are the two-legged variety." Without conscious thought, her hand moved to the healing wound above her eye.

The men exchanged another telling look.

"What?" Jenna asked.

Bernie once again broke the silence. "You're not like most people that I've met."

Jenna laughed. "I'll take that as a compliment."

He picked up a wrench and polished it. "You should."

"Now that we've bonded, you're not going to ask me to join your commune, are you?"

"Commune?" he asked, his confusion evident.

"Just checking," Jenna said, only half kidding.

"Oh, I get it." Bernie shook his head and chuckled. "This isn't the type of club that you can just join." He winked. "You don't have worry about anyone trying to *convert* you."

Jenna snorted. "Good to know." But she did wonder what type of club Bernie was referring to. All the clubs she knew about had special jackets, funny handshakes, or silly hats. She hadn't seen any of those things on the estate. Maybe they only trotted them out for special occasions? Or maybe they only wore them when outsiders weren't around?

Nic walked over to a coffee maker tucked between the shelves and poured himself a cup. "Thanks for making a fresh pot," he said, then added, "Want one?"

"Sure." Jenna smiled. "As long as you promise not to trip over anything while you're bringing it to me."

Nic smirked. "I'll do my best."

Jenna had forgotten all about making the coffee once she'd popped her head under the hood of the Bug and calculated the cost of repairs.

He poured her a cup and brought it over. "Figure out what's wrong with it yet?"

"Thanks." Jenna took the coffee from him. "Still working on it."

Nic brought the cup to his lips. "Need help?"

Jenna shook her head. "Nah, but thanks for the offer. I've worked on her so many times that I know this car inside and out. She doesn't keep her secrets for long."

She wasn't keeping secrets at all. The Bug had pretty much shouted that she was badly broken.

"If you have time later, I'd like to get your opinion on some diagnostics I ran on the truck," Bernie said.

"Yeah, I'd love to help," Jenna said. "Just let me finish

up here." It felt good to be included, to once again be part of a team.

Nic walked over to the Lincoln and set his coffee cup down. He didn't go back to work. Instead, he glanced at Jenna. His mouth opened and closed a couple of times, then his hand moved to the back of his neck. Nic rubbed the tendons absently.

The whole thing was odd and slightly unnerving. "What's up?" she asked.

"I was wondering." He bit his lip. "Do you have any plans tonight? If you do that's fine," Nic said in a rush. "But if you don't, I thought maybe we could...I mean if you're not busy."

Jenna blinked in surprise. *Was he asking her out?* She thought they'd just been teasing each other and hadn't taken the bantering seriously. Her gaze sharpened.

Nic was an attractive man with his sandy brown hair and dark blue eyes. He had the kind of disarming smile that drew people in and made them want to smile back. Any woman would be flattered to catch his attention—even Jenna, if only she hadn't...

Hadn't what? Met Aidan? Seen him naked? Been on the run? The truth sucked.

Jenna didn't want to hurt Nic's feelings. He'd been nothing but nice to her. At the same time, she couldn't in good conscience lead him on.

She was about to let him down easy, when a clack, clack, clack of claws scraped the concrete behind her. Jenna swiveled in time to see a huge black wolf come strolling into the garage.

It was so large that the top of its massive head reached her chest. Its ears were up. Alert. While its amber eyes watched her every move. It took another step, then hesitated.

A jolt of fear struck. Jenna's first instinct was to run from the pony-sized beast. The urge was followed by an equally strong impulse to stay put.

Bernie and Nic didn't say a word, but their shocked expressions spoke volumes.

So this wasn't something that happened every day.

"Is the wolf tame?" she asked softly. After all, it had walked into the garage filled with humans. Not typical behavior for a wild animal.

"Hardly!" Nic replied.

Jenna reached for a wrench, then visually examined the animal's mouth. She detected no foam or any other sign that would indicate that the wolf was rabid. She dropped the wrench back onto the tray of tools.

"Slowly come toward my voice." Nic cupped his hand, beckoning her to move away.

The hair on the wolf's back rose and he growled.

Jenna's legs locked. "Easy." Her hand trembled as she held it out and cooed quietly to calm the animal.

The wolf sniffed the air, then glanced at the men and slowly approached. Jenna continued speaking to it, her cadence low and soothing.

When her fingers were within an inch of the creature's massive muzzle, its tongue darted out and licked her hand.

She gasped in surprise. "Did you see that?"

"We saw it." There was an odd tone to Bernie's voice. One Jenna didn't recognize.

Encouraged by the wolf's response, Jenna inched closer, until she could touch the wolf's head. The creature flinched, but didn't shy away. Jenna took that as encouragement and petted the animal. She watched in amazement as his amber eyes closed.

"Oh my gosh! I can't believe this. Have you guys ever seen anything like this?" she whispered.

"No," they said in unison. "Never."

"This is amazing. I never thought in a million years I'd ever get the chance to do anything like this. I wish I could get a picture. He's beautiful. Truly magnificent."

Bernie and Nic didn't respond.

"Are you sure he's not tame?" she asked, unable to tear her gaze away. He sure seemed tame enough to Jenna.

"Positive," Nic said. There was tightness to his voice that hadn't been there before.

"Do you guys feed the wolves?" she asked.

"No, they hunt," Nic said. "If you don't stop petting him, he might just follow you home."

That would be a trick, since she didn't have a home. Still, Jenna couldn't hide her delight. "You know that only makes me want to pet him more, right?"

Nic took a step toward her. The wolf lowered its head, this time baring its teeth. Nic paled and stopped.

"I don't think he likes you," Jenna said.

Nic's color drained completely. His gaze dropped to the floor and he slowly backed away.

"I was only kidding," she said.

Without another word, Nic went back to work.

The wolf allowed Jenna to pet him one more time, then he left the garage, trotting off toward the woods.

"Pinch me. Seriously. I cannot believe that just happened," she said. "I'm pretty sure that's the coolest thing that has ever happened to me." She squealed like a little girl. "I've got to tell Aidan. He's never going to believe it."

Bernie shook his head, then went back to work.

"Come on, you guys. A wild wolf walks into the garage and you have nothing to say. Really?" She threw her arms up in exasperation. "I can't believe you are so nonchalant about what just happened. You act like this kind of thing happens all the time."

"It's not as unusual as you might think," Nic muttered.

"Whatever." Jenna walked to the door of the garage and paused. "Nic, about tonight..." Her voice trailed off.

He turned away from the engine, but didn't meet her gaze. Instead, he focused on the wrench in his hand. "You know what, I completely forgot that I had a meeting tonight. Can I take a rain check?"

That was odd, but Jenna was grateful for the excuse he gave her. "Sure." She nodded, then bolted out the door in search of Aidan. No doubt he would appreciate her wolf story.

Robert LaBeouf cut her off in the driveway before she reached the house. "Shouldn't you be at work?"

Jenna slowed, not wanting to get caught up in a conversation right now. "Not until this afternoon." She tried to move past him, but he stepped into her path. Clearly there was more on his mind than simple chitchat.

Robert straightened the sleeves on his impeccable suit and picked at invisible lint. "Any luck with the car?"

Jenna sighed and did her best to hide her impatience. "It's coming along." It would be a lot faster if she had the parts.

"So you'll be out of here soon?" he asked. "Before the weekend, perhaps?"

Why was he in such a hurry to get rid of her? "Should be," she said noncommittally. "Do you happen to know where Aidan is?"

Robert's jaw clenched. "Mr. Fortier is a busy man," he said. "He doesn't have time for you..." Robert sniffed. "Can I be frank?"

Like there was any way she could stop him. "By all means." Jenna grinned to hide her clenched teeth. Anything to speed up this unpleasant conversation.

"You're not his type," he said.

She stumbled back. Jenna struggled to come up with an appropriate response, but failed miserably, so she blurted the first thing that came to mind. "What makes you say that?"

He stared pointedly at the back patio. Several women milled around. A moment later Aidan strolled up the stairs. The women turned as one to greet him, bright smiles on their beautiful faces.

One woman stepped away from the others to approach Aidan. When she reached his side, she ran her hand down his back. It was an intimate gesture that indicated she had more than a passing familiarity with his body.

Aidan grinned at the woman and lovingly brushed a kiss across her cheek.

Jenna swallowed the lump that formed in her throat. How could she possibly compete with women like that? She glanced down at her grease-stained jeans and dirty hands. She couldn't.

Aidan's smile faded, when he caught sight of her in the driveway.

Pain raked her, but Jenna made sure not to show it. She wouldn't give either man the satisfaction of knowing that they'd hurt her. She stared at Aidan.

Was this the same man, who'd offered her assistance last night? The same one who'd stripped naked and stood beneath the moonlight in full view of everyone? The one who'd nearly kissed her? Last night, she'd convinced herself that he'd done all that for her benefit.

I'm such an idiot, she thought.

"As you can see, he's busy." Robert gestured to the women. "What did you want to tell him? I can relay a message if you like."

"That's okay," Jenna said, voice tight. "It's not important. I better go in and get ready for work."

Robert's dark eyes glimmered, then he glanced at his watch. "I thought you said you didn't have to work until this afternoon?" A shadow of a pleased smile crossed his lips, before his stern expression returned.

"I forgot that I had errands to run. If you'll excuse me." Jenna rushed off, before he could reply.

* * * * *

Robert watched her go. He needed to get rid of the human. She was distracting the Alpha from his duties to the pack. It proved once again that Aidan's blood was weak like his cousin's.

His lip curled in disgust.

How could anyone be attracted to vermin?

If René had won the Alpha challenge, he wouldn't have had to worry about the pack's future. René was easy to control, to lead. Robert thought for sure that the dumb wolf's size would give him an advantage in the fight. And it had, but not for long.

He'd underestimated Aidan.

Robert wouldn't make that mistake again.

He watched Jenna walk stiffly to the house, and couldn't help but smile.

If Aidan wouldn't run her off, then he would.

* * * * *

Jenna didn't understand the pain that she was experiencing. There was no logical reason for it. None whatsoever.

There was nothing going on between her and Aidan. *Nothing at all.* Better to know that now, than after it was too late.

She rubbed her chest to ease the ache and hurried toward the house. Jenna paused at the threshold and glanced back.

Robert LaBeouf still stood in the driveway. This time he was smiling at her. He'd dropped all pretenses.

She clenched her fists. Jenna had the sudden urge to stomp over there and punch him in the face. Maybe then, he'd lose that smug expression. But she wouldn't, because he wasn't worth it. None of them were.

With one last smirk, Robert strolled off toward the garage.

Something wet hit her cheek. Jenna violently scrubbed it away. "Knock it off," she muttered. "You've only known him for a few days."

She ran to her bedroom and shut the door, resting her back against the wood. Laughter filtered in from the outside.

The joyful sound slicing her deep.

How had she convinced herself that Aidan wasn't like her ex? Through the curtain sheers, her gaze swept the patio. The women were all flawless like they were auditioning for a photo shoot.

Aidan's dark head stood out above the crowd of females, a king holding court, a sheik surrounded by his harem. So there had been an element of truth to that story, too.

Jenna marched across the bedroom and snapped the thick drapes closed, plunging the room into darkness. It didn't entirely shut out the sound of the party, but at least she wouldn't have to watch Aidan take his pick of the women.

How could she have been so wrong about him?

She was determined now more than ever to get her interview. The wolf encounter would add a nice spin to the piece. Soon, she'd earn enough money to leave Breakbend. The thought should've filled her with excitement, but it didn't.

Aidan's not going to miss you. Given the bevy of beauties on the patio, he probably won't notice that you're gone.

Jenna wished that she could forget him as easily.

* * * * *

CHAPTER NINE

Aidan had *felt* Jenna's gaze on him. Even surrounded by all the female Weres, he could distinguish her from the others. When he'd glanced toward the driveway, he'd seen Robert and Jenna locked in a serious conversation.

A conversation only interrupted by Robert pointing to him. Jenna's body had tensed and her lush mouth had thinned. Their eyes met briefly. Long enough for him to see the pain, then it vanished. The connection he'd felt in the garage disappeared with it.

Jenna had been happy when he'd left her a few minutes ago. Ecstatic even. Aidan had taken a huge risk showing her his Other form.

He'd expected her to run away, but had hoped that she wouldn't. He should've known that Jenna would be brave given the courage she'd shown last night.

Aidan had sensed her fear, but her trepidation hadn't latest long. Jenna's curiosity was far stronger. When her fingers had sank into his fur, Aidan had nearly whimpered from the overwhelming wave of pleasure that came from her touch.

Even now, he could feel her stroking him, hear her

cooing softly in his ears. It took every fiber of his being not to rush to her side and confess that he and the wolf were one and the same.

A suicidal act if there ever was one.

Jenna had secrets. Secrets that were potentially dangerous to him and the pack. As Alpha, he couldn't overlook that. Of course, his secrets were even greater. Of that Aidan had no doubt. There was a reason why the Moonlight Kin and humans rarely mixed.

Of course, none of that explained what Robert was up to. Aidan made a mental note to find out, once his assistant returned from his visit into town.

* * * * *

Still angry with herself for getting emotionally attached so quickly, Jenna drove to town. The patio was clear by the time she left. No sign of Aidan or any of the model wannabes.

Unfortunately, that only made her mood worse. Jealousy scalded her insides, burning like acid. Where was he? Who was he with? What were they doing? And why weren't they still on the patio?

Carnal images flooded her mind. Tears threatened to return. "You're being ridiculous!"

Jenna pressed a button to roll down the window. Air rushed in, blowing the moisture away.

You're not his type. Robert's seething statement rang in her ears.

Judging by the appearance of those women, he'd been telling the truth. Jenna glanced in the rearview mirror. Other than the healing cut, she didn't look too bad.

A little underweight maybe, but that's what happened when you couldn't afford to eat everyday.

She examined her features carefully. Her green eyes were okay. Better with a little makeup. Her mouth was too wide, her lips a little too full. Nothing could be done about her crooked grin or strong jawline.

Face it, without plastic surgery you're never going to be model pretty.

Her gaze strayed to the road behind her. It was empty.

She felt the same way inside. Like part of her chest had been carved out and she'd been haphazardly sewn back together.

It dawned on Jenna that this was the first time she'd checked to see if someone was following her. She'd gone a whole day without looking. That had never happened before she'd met Aidan.

There was something about the man that made her feel safe and protected.

Jenna snorted in derision. "Don't get used to it." Today proved that wouldn't be smart.

Robert had made it clear that he expected her to be gone by the weekend. That didn't give her much time. Since he was Aidan's personal assistant, he could very well be speaking for his boss. What if that were the case? What if Aidan really didn't want her around? Pain returned, shoving the unreasonable jealousy aside.

Jenna pulled into Breakbend. This time she wasn't lucky enough to score a parking space in front of the paper. She found a spot in a lot a couple of blocks away. Jenna gathered her purse, then locked the Rover.

Busy shoppers had Main Street humming with energy. Several men wearing lure-covered fishing hats strolled down the sidewalks.

Must be some kind of tournament going on, she thought. Either that or the worst fashion show ever!

Jenna got her first inkling that something wasn't right, when she passed the coffee shop on the corner. It started with an itch between her shoulder blades. The itch became a crawl that crept down her spine. Carl's dogged pursuit had taught her never to ignore her instincts.

He was here.

It was only a matter of time before he caught up with her.

Jenna kept her pace even, taking care not to break stride or look around. Her gaze strayed to the windows that lined the storefronts. She searched the reflections for sudden movements, anything out of place.

It had to be Carl.

Who else could it be?

Once Carl caught her, he wouldn't go easy on her, especially after their last encounter. No doubt he didn't appreciate having his balls shoved into his intestines.

Somehow Jenna had to evade him for another day or two, until she could secure her interview and get her car repaired. Would be easy enough if she were in a city, but how could she hide in a town this small?

The paper came into view. Jenna passed the entrance. She saw Molly wave, then frown as she kept walking. She waited for the crowd of people to thicken, then she ducked down and darted into a side street.

The narrow lane gave her access to Puck Street, which ran parallel to Main, and went by the back of the Gazette building. When she came around the corner, Paul Welling was leaning against the back door, enjoying a long drag on a cigarette.

"What are you doing? Why didn't you use the front entrance?" He dropped the butt onto the ground and stubbed it out with his heel.

"Got turned around in the crowd. Missed the door. Lucky I found you," she said.

"Turned around in this town?" Paul scoffed, then his brown eyes narrowed. "How's the interview coming along?"

"Good." Her gaze strayed to the street. She didn't see Carl, but that didn't mean he wasn't there. "I should have it finished by tonight. In the meantime, is there any chance of getting an advance on my first paycheck?" She needed money to run.

Paul laughed. "After less than a week on the job?"

Jenna wasn't surprised by his answer, but it didn't hurt to ask. She was out of time. It was either get the interview tonight—or never.

"Let's go inside." Before Carl found out where she worked. He wouldn't hesitate to cause a scene. He'd made that clear, when he'd tried to abduct her. Jenna's hand touched the cut on her forehead. Never again.

* * * * *

CHAPTER TEN

Jenna's heart was in her throat. She'd stayed at work until five, long enough to make sure that Carl wouldn't wander in looking for her, then she'd snuck out the back door and made her way down side streets and alleys until she'd spotted the Rover.

She didn't immediately climb into the vehicle. Instead, Jenna watched the car and the streets for ten minutes before deciding it was clear enough to make a run for it. She jumped inside and sped off.

Her gaze flicked repeatedly to the rearview mirror, as she drove toward Aidan's estate. Twice she'd thought someone was following her, only to have them turn off on one of the streets leading out of town. Somewhere in Breakbend, Carl was searching for her.

I thought I'd have more time. Damn it, Ethan!

Jenna's sweaty palms slid across the steering wheel. It wasn't until she caught sight of the massive gates blocking the entrance to the estate that some of the tension eased in her shoulders.

She pressed a button and those imposing gates opened. Jenna glanced one last time at the barren road, then hit the gas, sending gravel spraying behind her as she barreled down the driveway. Shadows filled the woods as the sun sank below the horizon. Jenna kept seeing movement where there was none.

"Keep it together," she muttered, glancing once more in her rearview, even though she was safely behind the tall walls.

A black mass darted in front of her. Jenna screamed and jerked the wheel to the left to avoid hitting it. Something large thumped the bumper and sent her skidding out of control. The Rover fishtailed toward the trees.

Brush scraped the paint as she wrestled with the wheel. The front tires dipped, throwing Jenna sideways. Her head hit the driver's side window, stunning her. The seatbelt tightened, yanking her back against the seat.

She hit the breaks, but it was too late. The front of the SUV collided with the trunk of a pine tree. Glass shattered. Metal crunched. Then the airbag exploded in her face.

Dazed, Jenna glanced in the rearview mirror. A naked man lay on the other side of the driveway. That couldn't be right. She shook her head and squinted. His dark hair and muscular body came into focus and looked...*familiar*.

For a second, Jenna couldn't breathe, couldn't move, then adrenaline hit. "Aidan!" she cried.

Jenna struggled out of her seatbelt. What if he was hurt? What if he was... She couldn't even bring herself to think it. He had to be okay.

"Hang on, Aidan. I'm coming." Jenna threw the door open in a panic and fell onto the ground, her legs trembling too bad to support her. She pulled herself up, using the Rover for leverage. She had to get to Aidan.

Jenna scrambled up the short embankment and out of the woods. From here she should be able to see if he was breathing. She glanced across the road.

Aidan's body was gone.

It wasn't possible. She'd seen him. Did that mean he

wasn't hurt? Jenna glanced down the driveway, hoping to see him walking toward the house. There was no sign of Aidan.

Where did he go? Had he wandered into the woods?

Blood roared in her ears. Fear enveloped her. If Aidan had stumbled into the woods, then he was definitely hurt. She had to find him before the wolves did.

Jenna crossed the road, her gaze scanning the ground, searching for clues that might indicate which way he'd went.

"Aidan, where are you?" She turned in a circle, the trees blurring before her eyes. "Aidan!" Jenna couldn't lose him. Not like this. Not yet.

The shadows hid him at first. His black fur blended so well that she'd nearly stumbled over him. Her *wolf*. Lying next to the trees not far from where Aidan had been.

Or had he?

Had she really seen him?

Jenna wasn't sure.

Just how hard had she hit her head? She thought she'd only been momentarily stunned. Jenna felt the wound on her forehead, but other than being a little sore from the airbag, it didn't feel too bad.

Had she imagined the whole thing? Aidan had looked so real in the rearview mirror. She glanced across the driveway at the tilted SUV. The angle out the back wasn't perfect. It wouldn't give her the clearest view.

Jenna shook her head and looked down at the ground. Maybe she'd just wanted to see Aidan again. So much so that her brain had conjured him up for her. She didn't want to examine why too closely.

It dawned on her that he hadn't been wearing any clothes. Jenna groaned.

Terrific! Even during an accident, she couldn't escape thoughts of his naked body.

Jenna stared at the black wolf. The wolf stared back. She had hit something. Of that there was no doubt. Since Aidan wasn't here, it stood to reason that she'd struck her wolf.

She needed to make sure he was okay. If he wasn't, then somehow she'd coax him into a vehicle and get him to a vet. Jenna tried to imagine lifting over two hundred pounds of wolf into her car. No way could she do that without hurting him worse. He had to be okay.

"Easy, fella." Jenna held her hands out and kept her voice soothing. "How's my pretty boy?"

His ears perked up as he watched her approach. There didn't appear to be any visible injuries, but she wouldn't know for sure until she could examine him. Jenna kneeled as she neared the animal.

"Come here. I need to make sure that you're okay." She reached out and slowly felt his legs before making her way over his body, checking for tenderness.

There was no blood that she could see or feel. And nothing seemed to be swollen. Did that mean he was okay? Maybe she'd simply stunned him, too.

Please let him just be stunned.

"That's a good boy." Jenna carefully examined him again, making sure she hadn't missed anything. The wolf didn't whimper or flinch.

Relieved that he was unharmed and that it hadn't been Aidan that she'd hit, Jenna's composure shattered. She threw her arms around the wolf's neck and buried her face in his fur. The tears she'd held back released in a flood. All the pain and frustration she'd suppressed came bubbling out.

"I'm so sorry." Her shoulders shook as she cried. "I never wanted any of this to happen. I thought I'd have more time. But he's here," she said between hiccups. "I don't want to betray his trust...But I can't fight him without money." She sobbed. "He'll just keep coming...Won't ever stop...Maybe someday Aidan will forgive me."

The wolf licked the tears off her cheek, then swept his tongue over the wound on her forehead. Jenna could feel his muscles quiver beneath her hands, but he didn't try to pull away or try to bite her. She rubbed his head and ran her hand over his muzzle. "I'm glad you're okay."

He licked her hand.

She sniffed loudly and wiped her face with her sleeve. He couldn't understand a word she was saying, but that was okay. She'd just needed someone to listen.

"Thank you for letting me hold you. I'm glad you're all right." Jenna stroked the wolf's sides one last time, then slowly rose to her feet.

The wolf waited a moment, as if to make sure she was all right, then bounded into the woods.

Jenna watched him go, paying special attention to his strong legs. No limps. No favoring of sides. No whimpers of pain. She sighed. Thank goodness.

She walked back to the Rover and climbed behind the wheel. Jenna had no idea how she'd pay for the SUV's repairs, when she couldn't even cover the Bug's, but she'd get the money together somehow.

"Please start," she whispered.

The engine sputtered, then turned over. Jenna slipped the Rover into reverse. Twigs snapped and limbs creaked as she backed out of the woods and did a three point turn to get the SUV headed in the right direction. Jenna drove sedately down the rest of the way the driveway.

Aidan rushed outside when she reached the house.

Despite her encounter with the wolf, Jenna's gaze roamed over him, examining every inch. She needed to see for herself that he was unharmed. Her relief was palpable.

So much for keeping her emotions in check.

Aidan opened the driver's side door and pulled her into his arms.

Jenna allowed herself to sink into his warmth, feeling his strength beneath her fingertips. His chest rose and fell against her cheek. She could hear his powerful heartbeat, its steady cadence reassurance that he was in fact all right.

"Are you all right?" He brushed her hair away from her

face, his gaze carefully examining her.

People from the household gathered outside to see what the commotion was. They watched her and Aidan's exchange closely, their expressions registering various levels of surprise.

Uncomfortable with the growing audience, Jenna stiffened. "How did you—"

"Security cameras," Aidan answered before she could finish her question. "They saw everything. We were just about to come out and get you, when someone spotted the headlights. Are you sure that you're alright?" He moved her inside without waiting for an answer.

Robert stood in the doorway, his wiry frame ramrod straight. He took one look at the Rover and scowled at her. His frown deepened, when he noticed how tightly Aidan held her.

Jenna slipped out of Aidan's embrace. She felt guilty enough over having to betray him. She didn't need or want him to take care of her. His concern for her well-being only added to the heaping pile of self-loathing, growing inside of her.

Aidan didn't acknowledge the move. Instead, he countered it by wrapping his arm over her shoulder and maneuvering her up the stairs.

"Where are we going?" she asked.

"My room. I've called for our staff physician to meet us there."

His room. Warning bells went off in her head. Jenna didn't think going to Aidan's room was a good idea, stunned or not, but there was no deterring him. She had a feeling if she dug in her heels and refused, he'd pick her up and carry her.

Aidan threw open the double doors to what could only be described as a decadent master suite. Jenna took in the room in a glance.

It was no surprise that Aidan's bed garnered center stage

in the space. The massive sleigh frame carved from cherry wood appeared to be custom made. Jenna's suspicions were confirmed when she caught sight of the extra large mattresses.

Soft cream sheets met a mountain of pillows. Two matching side tables flanked the bed. There were books stacked on top of both.

Aidan was a reader.

Jenna wasn't sure why that surprised her or why it pleased her so much. She scanned the titles quickly, recognizing a few familiar names before her gaze was drawn to a set of dual French doors. The doors led out to what looked like a large balcony.

The perfect spot for the king to survey his kingdom, she thought. A soft knock interrupted her musings.

"Come in, Gabe." Aidan didn't look to see who was at the door.

A man with sandy blond hair and gold-rimmed glasses entered the room, carrying a brown leather bag. Jenna had never seen him before, but he seemed familiar with the space. He walked past them straight into Aidan's bathroom and set the bag on the counter. "Bring her in here."

Aidan guided Jenna into the bathroom.

"I can walk by myself you know?" she said.

Aidan's amber gaze assessed her. "You've no doubt bumped your head and had an airbag explode in your face. I want to make sure you're okay."

Several painful finger probes and a barrage of pointless questions later, Dr. Gabe declared that she didn't have a concussion. Jenna could've told him that.

The doctor gave her a couple of aspirin.

Jenna dry swallowed them.

He removed his latex gloves and tossed them into the trash, then closed his bag. His gaze returned to the healing wound on her forehead. "You should've had someone take a look at this right after it happened. It might've prevented scarring."

Scarring had been the least of her concerns. Jenna hadn't had the money to see a doctor. Nor had there been time when she was running away from Carl. She didn't have the money now either.

"I don't have health insurance," she said. Not an oddity in this day and time.

Dr. Gabe turned to Aidan. "She'll be fine. It's just a knock. Let me know if she gets sleepy or her speech slurs."

Jenna glared at him. "*She* can hear you. She's standing right here."

Gabe didn't spare her a glance as he waited for Aidan's response. "Stay close." He glanced at Jenna. "Never know when trouble might arrive."

* * * * *

CHAPTER ELEVEN

Aidan's heart continued to race in his chest. When he'd seen Jenna skid off the road into the woods, something inside him had shattered.

The bone deep sense of loss had struck him to the core and he could no longer ignore the growing connection between them or the need to find out where it would lead.

Terror was not a feeling Aidan was used to experiencing or one he cared to repeat. It didn't sit well with his wolf.

Thank goodness she'd been driving the Rover and not her vehicle or the accident could've been a lot worse.

She'd been crying so uncontrollably. Each tear had battered his Lycan soul. In his wolf form, Aidan had had difficulty following her conversation. Though he doubted that it would've made sense in his human form either, since she'd had her face buried in his side.

He'd caught enough to know that Jenna intended to betray him, but he still didn't understand why. The odd part was it didn't make him angry.

By rights, he should be furious with her. Instead, all he could think about was who had arrived in town?

Just the thought of Jenna around another male brought

out some very uncomfortable feelings. On a normal day, it was hard to fight his nature. This close to the full moon made it damn near impossible.

Jenna was in danger. Of that there was no doubt. Aidan had suspected as much, but her disjointed, tear-soaked confession proved it.

Someone was after her. Someone she feared. That same fear drove her now to do things she wouldn't normally do. His Alpha instincts quickly rose to the surface. The urge to protect what was his burned through his body. Aidan wanted to sink his claws into the threat and eviscerate it.

But he needed more information. He had to be able to identify the threat. Once he did that, Jenna wouldn't have to worry anymore. Now the question was, how would he ferret out the truth?

Demanding that she tell him everything would only drive Jenna away. She was stubborn to a fault. There was only one way forward. Aidan had to let her go through with her 'plan'. Whatever it may be. Convince her that he was falling for her ruse, then like any good wolf, he would pounce.

Aidan felt her gaze scroll over him. She'd been doing that ever since she had entered the house. He would've been flattered, if he didn't think there was more behind the look than plain lust.

"What are you looking for?" he asked.

She jumped and her voice squeaked. "What?"

Aidan tilted his head. "You keep looking at me with a funny expression on your face. What is it you're searching for?"

Jenna hesitated. "It's ridiculous."

He brushed a strand of hair away from her face. "Tell me anyway."

She bit her lip, drawing his gaze to her mouth. "It's going to sound crazy."

Aidan smiled. "Promise I won't laugh."

She took a deep breath. "For a moment back in the

woods, I thought I'd hit *you*."

Aidan didn't blink, didn't show any emotion at all. "Why would you think that?"

Jenna shook her head. "When I looked in the rearview mirror after the accident, I could've sworn I saw you lying by the side of the road. Obviously, I didn't. You're here. Unhurt. The accident scrambled my mind and somehow I incorporated all those wild stories I heard in town."

His brows rose.

She rubbed her arms, quelling the gooseflesh. "Told you it was crazy."

Aidan closed the distance between them. "There are a lot of things that cannot be easily explained away by logic. If you say that you saw me in the woods," he shrugged, "then maybe you did."

Jenna's lips flattened. "Don't patronize me. I know you weren't in the woods. I hit a wolf."

"Was he okay?" he asked.

She nodded. "I checked."

He waggled his eyebrows. "So you're saying that I look like a wolf?"

Jenna grinned. "When you look at me like that." She pointed at his face. "Yeah, you could do a passing impression."

"I'm flattered." Aidan held out his hand. Jenna hesitated, then slowly took it. Her fingers were so fragile beneath his. One squeeze would crush every bone in her hand to dust. Aidan closed his fingers around hers and led her out of the room.

"Sorry about the Rover," she whispered. "I'll pay for the repairs. In fact, I'll do the work myself to make sure it's done right."

"It's not important. The vehicle is insured." Aidan led her down the stairs.

She pulled back. "Please stop being so nice."

Aidan snorted. "No one has ever accused me of that."

She rolled her eyes. "Then they don't know you very well."

Aidan's chest filled with warmth. He liked that she thought he was nice. Liked doing nice things for her, if it got him a smile.

"I'm hungry." And he was, just not for food. The taste of her sweet skin still lingered on Aidan's tongue, burning its way through his body in a rush. He desperately wanted another taste, a far more intimate taste.

His wolf surfaced. Aidan felt his shaft stir behind his zipper. He waited, but it didn't go down. If anything, he grew even harder.

Fine! Aidan growled at his wolf. *You'll get your way this one time, and one time only.* He was desperate enough to make a deal with the devil, if it meant the end of his 'affliction'. *Tonight I'll have sex with her and prove to you once and for all that she's not the one.*

His wolf yipped with excitement.

After we've had her, you'll change your mind. You will see that there's nothing remarkable about humans, then we can get back to the business of sorting through the Werewomen. Do we have a deal?

In his head, Aidan heard his wolf howl.

He escorted Jenna to her room. "Take a quick shower and we'll head into town."

"Town?" Jenna's eyes widened and she pulled her hand away. "Why would you want to go there?"

"To get something to eat," he said slowly.

Her scent turned bitter. "Why not eat here?" Panic squeezed her voice, making the pitch higher.

"I eat here most nights. I'm in the mood for something different." That was the absolute truth. His heated gaze slid over her, then Aidan paused. "You told me that you felt fine. Do I need to call Gabe back?"

* * * * *

"No! I mean. I am fine. Still a little shaken from the accident." Jenna swallowed hard. The change in Aidan's behavior toward her had her head spinning. Things were suddenly moving too fast.

Jenna wasn't oblivious. She'd noticed there was sexual tension between them, albeit muted. There was nothing dampening it now. It was like the accident had removed a barrier. She could now see the full brunt of his desire.

Aidan's intense focus thrilled her and frightened her. Jenna wasn't convinced she could handle the heat without being consumed, which was why she found herself trying to bow out.

"Doubt I'd be very good company tonight," she said.

Aidan was giving her the perfect opportunity to interview him, but the offer came with strings. Strings that threatened to bind her, making escape impossible.

Part of Jenna ached to give in. It had been so long since she'd *touched* another human being, or been held all night in someone's arms. Her skin prickled. If she concentrated, she could almost feel the warmth of his hands on her body. But there were other things to consider beyond primal needs.

Carl's pugnacious face flashed in her mind.

The thought of running into him drove the heat from her body, sobering her. She had no idea what Carl would do. Would he start a fight? Try to drag her into his car like the last time?

Jenna didn't want Aidan in the line of fire. Better to drive a wedge between them now, than to have harm come to him. This wasn't his fight. It was hers.

"It's just a casual dinner. I'm not looking to be entertained." Aidan seemed unnaturally calm. Like accidents, house calls, and strangers disrupting his life were the norm around this place.

She took a different tack. One Jenna was sure would hit its mark. "Wouldn't you prefer one of your women to go with you? No doubt any one of them would jump at the chance." The snap in her voice surprised her. All she'd wanted to do was douse the rising flames, but somehow her tone had had the opposite effect.

Aidan's amber eyes appeared to glow and he looked unduly pleased. He didn't dispute her claim. How could he? She'd seen the models with her own eyes. He also didn't gloat, but then again, he didn't need to. He was well aware of how appealing he was to the opposite sex. The only thing that had changed was now he knew she wasn't immune to his charm.

"I want you," Aidan paused, "to join me tonight."

His words seared her flesh, exposing her vulnerability. She wasn't clueless. She hadn't missed the double-entendre. In desperation, Jenna tried one last time to dissuade him.

"If you're looking to add to your harem, then you'd better look elsewhere."

A nerve in Aidan's jaw started to tic. "I do not have nor have I ever had a harem. They're not culturally relevant for me and the concept is outdated. Don't you think?" he continued. "What I do have is a lot of responsibility. More responsibility than you could ever imagine."

Jenna massaged her temple. This wasn't working like she'd hoped. The barb had hit too close and clearly wounded him. She hadn't meant to hurt him. She only wanted to prevent him from making a mistake. And perhaps stop herself at the same time.

"I'm sorry," she said. "I didn't mean it like that." She had, but said aloud it sounded mega-bitchy. Not at all like she'd intended. "I have a bit of a headache."

Aidan's gaze bored through her. "Perhaps we should dine some other time, when you're feeling more up to it." He turned to leave.

"No." Jenna stopped him.

This was her last chance to get that interview, and the last opportunity to be held in his arms. There wouldn't be another. She stared at him. Saw the heat. Saw the offer in his eyes. If she wanted more, Aidan made it clear he'd oblige. Did she dare accept?

"I'll get cleaned up and be out in thirty," she said.

Aidan arched a brow.

"It won't take me long." Jenna planned to pack once she showered. After dinner, Aidan might very well toss her out of his house. She wanted to be ready for every contingency.

And just where do you think you'll go without a car? You wrecked the one he gave you to drive. It's not like he's going to loan you another.

Her shoulders slumped. She'd forgotten all about the Bug. "Maybe I should go check on my car before we leave." Could she somehow rig it to run? Doubtful. All she had to do was make it to the next town. Jenna supposed she could hitchhike again, but that was a last resort.

Aidan shook his head. "Not necessary. I had your vehicle repaired. I'd planned to surprise you, when you got home from work."

Jenna's heart sank. He was killing her with kindness, one act at a time. She didn't think she'd survive another good deed. Aidan was making it so hard to betray him.

"When did you find the time?" she asked.

"Nic looked it over the night it was towed in. After he met you, he sent Josh into the city for parts."

"So that's the errand he was running?" She shook her head.

Aidan nodded. "Don't be upset. Nic took care of the repairs personally as a favor to me," he said.

There was something about his tone that gave Jenna pause. Why would Nic owe Aidan a favor? The guy worked for him.

"I should probably go out and thank him," she said. "Is he still in the garage?"

Aidan caught her arm, his thumb brushing gently over her skin. "There's no need. He was honored to help."

"Honored?" She let her incredulity show.

"When you speak to him later, you'll see. For now, get ready. My hunger is growing by the second. Soon I'll be ravenous and we might not make it to the restaurant." Heat poured off his body, causing his wild scent to deepen. The woodsy spice perfumed the air, making her feel giddy.

Thoughts of food deserted her. Despite a slight headache, something inside Jenna flared to life, answering the unspoken question she saw in his eyes. Was she prepared to meet the inferno head on? If not now, when would she get another chance?

"I better hurry." She hiked her thumb over her shoulder toward her room.

"You do that." Aidan's feral grin curled her toes and sent a thrill tripping down her spine. He glanced at his watch, then leaned in next to her ear. His warm breath brushed the skin, then he inhaled. "If you're not out in twenty-five minutes, I'm coming in after you." Threat. And a promise.

* * * * *

Chapter Twelve

The drive into town was a strange combination of tension and heightened awareness. The knot in Jenna's stomach grew the closer they got.

Was she going to go through with this? Could she really betray Aidan after all he'd done for her? If she did, that would make her no better than Ethan. The thought made her skin crawl.

She scanned the streets searching for Carl. Ethan's lackey had to be here somewhere, lurking in the darkness like a troll.

"One problem at a time," Jenna muttered to herself.

Aidan looked at her, but said nothing.

A spot opened up like it had been waiting for them. Aidan pulled the luxury sedan into the spot and parked. Jenna reached for the door handle.

"Sit tight." He got out and walked around the front of the car to open her door.

No one could fault him on his manners.

"This really isn't necessary." Jenna glanced up and down the sidewalk. Where was he? There was no sign of Carl, but she was determined to remain vigilant.

Aidan smiled. "We're celebrating the repair of your vehicle, remember?"

Jenna stopped. "About that, I know I keep saying this, but I will pay you back for parts and labor. It might take me a while, but I am good for it."

He rested his hand on the small of her back and led her into a cozy restaurant that only had ten tables. Candles fluttered as he opened the door and stepped aside for her to enter.

"Mr. Fortier, how lovely to see you." An older man rushed forward to greet them. "It's been a long time."

Aidan shook his hand. "Too long, Francis. Do you have my table?"

The man's brown eyes crinkled. "But of course." He led them toward the back of the room into the corner. Francis snapped his fingers and one of the bus boys rushed out carrying a table. He set it down and moved back as another one brought out two chairs. Within seconds the table was set and ready for them to dine.

Aidan signaled Francis to back away. "Allow me." He held Jenna's chair out and waited for her to take a seat.

Jenna gave him a small smile and sat. Could she feel any worse? She didn't think so. How could she have ever believed that Aidan was anything like Ethan?

He took his seat across from her, angling the chair until his back was against the wall, then perused the wine list. "Do you have a preference?"

"Red."

"Red it is." Aidan closed the menu and ordered a bottle.

Jenna waited until the waiter poured the wine, then asked her first question. "Are you originally from Breakbend?"

"No, I just like the area. There are a lot of woods to get lost in," he said.

"You like getting lost in the woods?"

He smiled. "On occasion. Keeps my instincts sharp. What about you? Where are you from?"

"I grew up all over," she deflected.

People like Aidan wouldn't understand how she grew up. Wouldn't understand what it was like to go without, to be neglected, to have to lock your door at night to prevent one of your many 'fathers' from coming in. Jenna lifted the glass of wine to her lips and took a deep swallow to keep from choking on the memories.

"So what made you want to keep wolves?" she asked.

He stared at her, his expression inscrutable. "They're not bees. I don't so much keep them as allow them to roam on my land."

"If that's the case, how did you tame them?" she asked.

"I didn't." Aidan paused their conversation while the waiter took their order. When that was finished, he continued. "Wolves sense things on a deeper level than people. They can smell your fear, your intentions, and especially your pain." He gave the last word added emphasis.

Jenna shifted in her seat. "Do you have family nearby?"

Aidan shook his head and laughed to himself. "I *always* have family around. It's difficult to find a moment to myself. What about you?"

"No, no family."

The answer surprised him.

Jenna opened her mouth to ask her next 'interview' question.

Aidan held up his hand to stop her. "Don't you want to write this down for accuracy's sake?" He sat back. "I'll wait until you get your notebook out of your purse."

Blood rushed to her face until the pressure threatened to pop her ears off. How was it possible to feel so hot and so cold at the same time?

Jenna considered denying his assertion, but she couldn't. What was the point? She'd never been the type of person to betray another. It just wasn't in her nature.

Jenna thought she could get the interview without him

knowing, but she had a feeling she would've confessed even if Aidan hadn't seen through her deception.

The wine in her stomach turned to vinegar. "I'm sorry." Jenna placed her napkin on the table and rose to her feet.

"Where do you think you're going?" Aidan kept his seat and casually swirled the wine around in his glass.

"I thought now that you caught me, you'd want to..." The words died on her lips.

"Please sit down, Jenna. We need to talk." Aidan waited for her to take her seat. "But first tell me why you were trying to get an interview."

Jenna's chin dropped. "I needed the money." She sighed. "I have some legal issues that I have to take care of. The situation is embarrassing and I'd rather not go into detail. Suffice to say, landing an interview with you would go a long way toward hiring the experts that I need."

"So you're not just trying to further your journalism career?"

She scoffed and glanced around to make sure no one had heard her. "I'm a mechanic, Aidan, not a journalist. This is just a job to pay the bills. My passion is cars. Running into you was a coincidence."

Aidan took a sip of wine. "Why didn't you just say so?"

Jenna sat up. While she spoke, she straightened the silverware in front of her. "I didn't know how. You were being so nice. At first I was suspicious. People like you aren't normally—"

"People like me?" He cut her off with an arched brow.

"You know what I mean." She sighed. "People in your income bracket aren't normally philanthropic toward individuals."

"True," he said. "So what changed?"

My feelings for you, she wanted to say, but didn't dare.

Cars drifted by the window down the darkened street. People strolled along the sidewalks. Still no sign of Carl, but he was out there somewhere. He wasn't about to stop pursuing her.

"I ran out of time," Jenna said.

Their food arrived. The aroma of rich tomato meat sauce filled the air. The waiter placed a basket of fresh baked breadsticks in the center of the table. The food looked great. Smelled great. But Jenna was no longer hungry.

Aidan picked up his fork and stared at her expectantly. "The food here is fabulous. Don't let it go to waste."

Jenna blew out a heavy breath and picked up her fork. "When we get back, I'll get my things and leave."

He took a bite and chewed his pasta slowly, seeming to mull over her words. Once he swallowed, he asked, "Why would you do that?"

"I know you have something going on over the weekend and honestly, I feel awful for betraying your trust. I think it's best if I just pack up and move on."

"Best for whom?" Before she could respond, he said, "Eat, we'll discuss trust later."

* * * * *

Chapter Thirteen

Someone was watching them.

Aidan had been distracted by Jenna's ripe and ever-changing scent. The sensual aromas made him want to push his plate of pasta aside and eat her instead. That overwhelming desire was why he hadn't immediately heard the soft clicks. Now the noise had his full attention.

It took him a moment to locate the source of the sound. Once he did, his anger surfaced.

Was photographic evidence also part of her 'plan'? He kept calm, even though all he wanted to do was run outside and confront the enemy.

"Did the interview I gave you include a photo spread?" He'd know the second she lied.

Jenna's brow furrowed. "Don't think so." She picked up her napkin and dabbed the side of her mouth. "If it did, then the editor didn't let me know about it. I could ask the paper to cover the cost of a photographer, if you'd like. Why do you ask?"

"Because I'm not fond of having my picture taken." It was dangerous for Lycans given their slow aging process and long lives.

"Okay, I understand. I'll let Paul Welling know," Jenna replied, undisturbed by his response. She picked up her fork and took another bite. Her scent never wavered.

She was telling the truth.

So who was watching them? And why take the pictures? And did this have anything to do with why Jenna was so scared?

Aidan spotted movement in the alley across the street. The man hadn't concealed himself well enough. If he had, Aidan might not have detected him, which meant he wasn't dealing with someone used to hunting Lycans.

The lighting in the restaurant made it difficult to make out the man's features, but Aidan could see he was a burly man. He needed to get the man's scent before it faded, then there wouldn't be anyplace for him to hide.

Their spy was gone by the time dinner drew to a close. Aidan waited for Jenna to finish her coffee. She'd gotten her interview, but hadn't spilled all her secrets yet.

Aidan needed a better setting, a more private one, before they continued their conversation. Fortunately for him, there were other ways, more pleasurable ways to obtain the information. Once he had her safely sequestered, he'd get his answers. Aidan would find out who the man across the street was and how he factored into the picture.

"Ready?" he asked.

Jenna nodded. "Thank you again for the interview. You've saved my life."

Did she mean that figuratively or literally?

"It's still early. How about we go for a stroll once we get back to the compound?" he asked.

"I could stand to work off some of these calories." Jenna glanced at her watch. "But are you sure it's safe?"

"Safe?"

"With the wolves in the woods?"

"Ah," he said. "They won't bother us."

"Wouldn't be too sure. The black one and I have bonded.

He doesn't like it when other people are near me."

Aidan bit back a grin. "Wolves are very territorial, but then again, so am I." He allowed his gaze to roam over her body. He planned to help her work off every calorie she ingested—after their walk.

Jenna blushed.

Aidan quickly paid for the meal, then walked around the table. His hands rested lightly on her shoulders before sliding to the back of the chair. He gently pulled it out. "I can't wait to see you in the moonlight." And neither could his wolf.

* * * * *

He made it sound like he couldn't wait to see her naked. Jenna could think of a lot of reasons taking a walk was a bad idea. The biggest of all was Aidan himself.

For the first twenty minutes of the dinner, she'd been riddled with guilt and terrified that Carl would show up. Sometime during the meal, she'd relaxed. Her guilt had abated and the sexual tension had returned. The heat had continued to build until Jenna half expected to see smoke rising from her skin.

She didn't think she'd make it through a walk without jumping him. Heck, Jenna wasn't convinced she'd make it to the car.

She stood, doing her level best to avoid eye contact. It had been the eye contact that had sucked her in, in the first place.

Aidan's amber gaze trapped her, immobilizing her as effectively as the real thick substance. He had a way of staring that made her believe she was the most important person on the planet. Jenna could see how a woman could easily become addicted.

He flashed her a devastating grin that sent butterflies aloft in her stomach. "Let's go."

Jenna scanned the sidewalks before she stepped outside.

"Looking for someone?" he asked.

She shook her head. "No, it's habit. I like to be aware of my surroundings."

"Smart woman." Aidan opened the car door for her and waited for Jenna to climb inside. Before he shut the door, he said, "Excuse me for a moment."

Jenna watched him dart across the street and slip between two buildings. Where was he going? What was he doing?

Aidan didn't strike her as the kind of guy who urinated in public, not when there was a perfectly good restroom in the restaurant. He was back before she could ponder it further.

He opened the car door and climbed in. "All set?"

"What were you doing in the alley?" she asked.

"I needed to check something really quick."

"What?" she asked.

"Nic thought he lost his wallet over there," he said.

Jenna glanced at the dark alley. "You probably need a flashlight to find it, unless it glows in the dark."

"True." Aidan's amber eyes glittered with amusement. "Fortunately, I discovered everything I needed to know."

* * * * *

Aidan had hoped that the house would be quiet by the time they returned from dinner. He should've known better. The estate bustled with activity as everyone prepared for the moon run.

He pulled the car in front of the house, then opened the door for Jenna. Once he helped her out, Aidan popped the trunk and grabbed a blanket that had been tucked in the back. "I think we picked a good night to go for a walk."

Jenna raised a brow at the blanket, but didn't comment. She glanced at the house. "What's going on?"

"Prep for the weekend festivities," he replied. "Come." Aidan shoved the blanket under his arm and took her hand.

He led her around the back of the house and across the yard. "I'd like to show you one of my favorite spots."

She smiled.

"You warm enough?" He examined her sweater, then checked her feet. The shoes she had on were practical like the woman. No need to go in and change, but he wanted her to be comfortable.

"It's a mild night. I should be fine. The walk will get the blood pumping," she said. "And if it doesn't, I could always use the blanket under your arm. That is why you brought it, isn't it?" Her green eyes sparkled with mirth.

Aidan thought it best to keep his mouth shut. Any answer he gave would either incur her wrath or reveal his intentions. He walked them into the woods.

"Don't we need a flashlight?" Jenna asked.

"Not with the moon so full above us. Give your eyes time to adjust." Aidan guided them down a rarely used path that wound its way through the woods, eventually buffeting a small creek.

"This is beautiful. You were right. I can see just fine." She tripped. "Well, good enough anyway."

Aidan navigated around stones and toppled limbs, making sure that Jenna didn't stumble again. "It's not far now."

The sound of rushing water grew louder. The damp scent of moist leaves mingled with the forest around them. The trees parted and they stepped into a small clearing.

Moonlight glistened off the rippling pool, its pale light shimmering like diamonds tossed onto a velvet screen.

* * * * *

Jenna gasped.

The pristine scene didn't look real. "Is this man-made?"

Aidan shook his head. "No, that's why I love it."

"It's beautiful," she said. "I've never seen anything like

it. How did you find it?"

Aidan glanced at her, then tilted his chin up until he was staring at the moon. "I spend a lot of time in the woods. Every chance I get. I found it on one of my many outings."

She looked around, drinking in the primeval beauty of the place. "Does anyone else know about it?"

"Probably, but they don't come here," he said.

"Why?" she asked, unable to tear her gaze away from his upturned face. The man was truly stunning. In the moonlight, with shadows delineating his features, he looked wild, untamed, barely human, as he basked in the pale light.

"Because this is my special spot. My favorite spot," he said, as if that should explain everything. He spread the blanket out on the ground.

Jenna shook her head, surprised that his arrogance only added to his attraction. "Do you ever go swimming here?"

Aidan's chin dropped and their eyes met. "Are you offering?"

"It would probably be a little cold for me." Though the idea was tempting, since neither of them had a swimsuit.

"I could keep you warm," he whispered.

And just like that, the temperature around them shot up. At least it felt like it to Jenna. Her mind immediately recalled his naked body, standing by the woods. She bit her lip and looked away, afraid that if she met his amber gaze, she'd be lost.

Aidan's finger hooked her chin and gently brought it around, until she had no choice but to look at him. "We won't do anything you don't want to do," he said.

That was the problem. Right now, her good judgment had its fingers stuck in its ears and was yelling, 'la, la, la, I don't hear you'.

When she didn't respond, Aidan dipped his head. Their mouths were now but a breath apart. The heat between them radiated with the fires of a thousand suns. Jenna couldn't focus. Her mind fogged as she stared at his sensual lips.

"You expect too much of me." Aidan groaned and closed the distance between them. Their lips met, then fused together.

Jenna's world tilted and began to spin. He slid his tongue along the seam of her mouth, silently begging for entrance.

He didn't have to ask twice.

Fire exploded inside of Jenna. Months of avoiding human contact came rushing to the forefront. She opened her mouth and let Aidan explore. Her fingers flitted against his arms, then tightened.

Jenna clamped onto Aidan's biceps and pulled him closer. The tone of the kiss changed as she let her passions loose to take over. Growling reached her ears, but Jenna couldn't tell if it was coming from her throat or Aidan's.

He tightened his grip on her and eased her onto the ground. The ferns and grass beneath the blanket cushioned Jenna, as Aidan deepened their embrace. His hand moved from her waist up her ribcage, stopping short of the soft swell of her breast.

Jenna ached for him to touch her. A tactile creature deprived for too long, she was greedy for every touch, every taste. Aidan continued to tease her flesh, while he fed from her mouth. Jenna arched beneath him, her grip tightened as fire streaked through her, leaving her breathless.

She gasped. "Aidan, please."

His big palm cupped her and squeezed.

Jenna jolted, feeling the sensation all the way to her toes. Aidan kneaded her breast, while he plucked at her nipple. He tore his mouth away from hers and shoved his hands up her shirt, lifting the material as he did so, exposing her to the night air.

Aidan lowered his head and kissed her stomach, his tongue making lazy circles over her skin. The moisture caused gooseflesh to rise, but Jenna wasn't cold. She was spontaneously combusting, burning from the inside out.

He continued to feast on her flesh, nibbling and licking

his way around her nipples, never removing her bra. Jenna couldn't stay still. She writhed, trying to get closer. She needed him to touch her. All of her.

Eventually his teasing was too much. Jenna grasped his head, sinking her fingers into his hair, and yanked his face forward.

Aidan's nose sank into the crevice between her breasts. Jenna thought she felt him smile, but she was too far gone to look down and see. Aidan bit down on the clasp, holding her bra together. The material parted and her breasts spilled out.

He inhaled, his big body shaking as he did so. "You are magnificent," he murmured, then ran his tongue over her bare skin.

Jenna quivered.

Aidan sucked on one nipple, while he palmed the other, making happy noises in the back of his throat. Each lick, each swirl, each tug of his mouth made the sensitive spot between her legs throb.

He hadn't even touched her there yet. Jenna was afraid she'd explode before he did.

"Aidan," she gasped.

* * * * *

Aidan shivered as his name fell from Jenna's lips. How many hours had he imagined this moment? This woman naked beneath him? His fantasies failed by comparison to the reality. Jenna's skin was like silk under his mouth.

He sucked in, swirling his tongue around the kernelled flesh. It hardened even more. Aidan closed his eyes in ecstasy. He could feast on her for hours.

The hotter she got, the more musky and delicious she smelled to him. He couldn't wait to bury his face between her legs and taste her essence.

He shuddered again, trying to keep his wolf in check. He'd promised him that he'd let him take her, but his control was hanging on by a hair.

Aidan reluctantly released her and quickly slipped his jacket off and tugged his shirt over his head. Jenna's eyes widened as she watched, then she smiled.

Her fingers brushed his chest. "You are amazing. Almost unreal in the moonlight."

He grinned. "Glad you think so."

"I do." She ran her hands along the ridges of muscle that covered his abdomen.

"Your turn." Aidan helped her sit up, so he could finish taking her shirt off.

Jenna's gaze met his. "Are we really going to do this?"

Goddess, he hoped so. Aidan didn't think he'd survive, if she stopped things now. But he wouldn't pressure her. He needed her to come willingly to him. To his wolf. He had to prove to it that she wasn't his bondmate.

If you do this there will be no turning back, a little voice whispered in his head. *There will be consequences.*

Aidan knew it was the truth, but right now he didn't care. He was tired of always doing the right thing. Just this once, Aidan wanted something for himself—for his wolf.

He rested his forehead against hers. "We can stop whenever you like." He hesitated. "Do you want to stop?"

Jenna shook her head. "Do you?"

"Hell no!"

She giggled.

Aidan latched onto her mouth and didn't stop kissing her until she was breathless. His body couldn't get much harder. Even his shaft was straining to be free.

Don't fail me. It was a plea and a prayer.

Soft breasts brushed his hard chest, causing Aidan to quake.

Every sensation felt new, fresh, and unique.

His hands trembled as he reached for the zipper on her pants. "Last chance," he murmured. It was the truth. Aidan had a feeling that once he claimed her body, there'd be no escape for either one of them.

* * * * *

Words evaded Jenna. She existed in a world of sensation. Aidan's hard chest abraded hers, making her nipples throb. His hands seemed to be everywhere at once, coaxing, inflaming, and enticing. The firm ridge of his shaft, brushed her stomach, leaving her aquiver.

She reached between their bodies and grasped him through his jeans, giving him the answer to his question. Aidan moaned and his hips rocked forward.

"Do that again," he hissed.

Jenna did, relishing in the power she held over him, over his beautiful granite-hard body. She released the button on his pants and slid the zipper down. He did the same to her. Jenna wiggled out of her denims, then hooked her foot in his waistband.

Aidan snagged a condom out of his pocket, before Jenna pushed his pants down, then kicked his clothes away. They were both sprawled on the ground in their underwear. There was a sharp rip and Jenna saw Aidan toss her black panties aside.

"That's not fair." She laughed.

"True, but it's effective," he said.

"What about yours?" she asked.

"In a minute." His eyes shimmered like molten gold in the moonlight. "First I want to feast." Aidan slid down her body. He used his broad shoulders to part her thighs, then he looked at her and gave her a feral grin.

Jenna's eyes rolled back in her head at the first swipe of his tongue and her whole body trembled. The look of sheer concentration on his face as he devoured her was enough to undo her.

Add to that his innate oral skills and you had a deadly combination. Jenna's thighs shook as he flicked and swirled, then plunged inside her only to return after a moment to repeat the whole process again.

She clawed at the ground. Her body quaked with the need for release, but Aidan wouldn't give it to her. He continued to tongue, taste, and tease her hidden folds, savoring her.

"Aidan!" she cried out, both in warning and desperation.

Her hips rocked as she sought that final connection, the final piece that would send her sailing into oblivion. Just when release was within reach, he stopped.

Jenna growled and slammed her fists onto the ground. "Don't you dare."

Aidan wiped his mouth with his discarded shirt and rose above her. "I'm not going to leave you hanging." He removed his underwear. His large shaft bowed under the weight of his erection, as he rolled a condom on. "I want you to take me with you."

He positioned his flushed crown at her soaking entrance, then scraped his thumb over the throbbing bundle of nerves at her apex.

Jenna screamed as her orgasm ripped through her body. The sound was followed by a deep moan as Aidan thrust, burying himself to the hilt inside of her. The conflicting sensations prolonged her release and sent another one rippling through her.

She'd never felt so full, so stuffed in her life. Aidan had looked big from a distance, but up close the man was massive in every way possible. Jenna gulped in air, as her body struggled to adjust.

* * * * *

Aidan squeezed his eyes closed and tried valiantly to breathe. Jenna's body gripped his shaft like a vise. It was heaven and hell at the same time. She was tight, so blissfully tight. Nothing had ever felt better.

Relief flooded him. He was whole. Healed from his

affliction. His body was working. He'd been so afraid that it wouldn't. That it would fail him again. Afraid that his wolf would change its mind at the last second and abandon him.

Aidan wasn't sure what he would've done, if his body hadn't responded. He pushed the horrifying thought aside. Everything was okay. Better than okay. It was great! Now he just needed to move. But he couldn't. Not until Jenna was ready.

Aidan grit his teeth. Sweat broke out over his body, while her channel continued to pulse. It took another minute or so for her breathing to return to normal. By then, Aidan was in agony.

"Let me know, if you need me to stop." He rocked his hips back.

Her lashes rose, but her passion-filled gaze remained unfocused. She didn't speak. Instead, Jenna pulled his mouth down to hers and kissed him. Relief overwhelmed him and Aidan let go, allowing her to pull him under.

His hips jerked, sending his shaft burrowing inside of her.

Jenna moaned and deepened the embrace.

Thank Goddess! Aidan thrust again. She felt so perfect, so utterly right. Their bodies fused and melded, coming apart and together in perfect synchronicity. He couldn't tell where he ended and Jenna began.

His wolf struggled to the surface, until it stared out through his eyes. Aidan's mouth began to water and his teeth lengthened.

No! He screamed in his head. *You're wrong!*

His wolf snorted, then snapped at him.

With the moon nearly full, there was no stopping the beast.

Jenna's knees grasped his hips and she locked her feet around him, not realizing the danger she was in. Her hands continued to explore his shoulders and back, while her lips found his earlobe.

Don't bite me. Please don't bite me. Aidan pleaded, but

not a word came out of his throat. He was beyond speech.

Jenna latched onto his earlobe and nibbled. Aidan grew even harder and his thrusts became more primal. His lips found the curve of Jenna's neck where it met her shoulder. He licked the spot, numbing it. The salt of her skin exploded on his tongue, yet he couldn't stop.

Aidan's shaft continued to grow and expand, until he burst out of the condom and filled every inch of Jenna's channel. He knew what it meant. It was what his wolf had been telling him all along.

He should've been terrified, but Aidan wasn't. No doubt later he would be. But right now, the only feeling he could muster was *relief*.

Jenna's hips canted and she mewed. Aidan thrust harder, though it was difficult to do so locked so tightly within her body. He shook, rocked by the first of what would be many orgasms tonight.

The movement swept Jenna up and took her with him. She screamed. Her eyes rolled back in her head and her body convulsed with pleasure.

The sound her unrestrained release made Aidan's wolf howl with joy. His baying increased in volume, as Aidan leaned over to nuzzle Jenna's neck. He licked her one more time, then opened his mouth wide.

"I'm sorry," he said, "but the decision is out of my hands."

Aidan bit down, breaking the skin. Her salty sweet blood filled his mouth, drowning his senses. He swallowed, drinking her in. Aidan had never tasted anything so delicious, so powerful. And she was his.

His for all eternity.

He lifted his head and bellowed, announcing the claiming of his bondmate to the moon. Jenna whimpered, but her eyes never opened.

Blood dripped from Aidan's chin onto the ground. He buried his face in her neck and cleaned her. He could remove most of the blood, but his mark would remain for all to see.

He kissed the spot. Jenna sighed, but didn't shy away. It didn't matter. Fate had already sealed all the exits.

* * * * *

Chapter Fourteen

Jenna snuggled deeper under the covers, relishing the softness of the bedding. A plush pillow cradled her head and her body ached in a deliciously decadent way. Memories of the previous night filled her head.

Aidan had been insatiable. She didn't know anyone past the age of sixteen who could recover so quickly. He'd had her six more times before Jenna had collapsed from exhaustion.

Until last night, she'd never known that a powerful orgasm could make someone faint from pleasure overload. It proved once again that she'd been dating the wrong men.

As if she needed more proof.

Jenna grinned and cracked an eye open. Her smile slowly faded. The room didn't look right.

The familiar dresser that sat against the wall was gone. It had been replaced by a heavy wood piece that stood at least a foot and a half taller. The walls were also a darker color cream.

She glanced over. The spot beside her was empty. The sheets cool to the touch. Her attention was drawn to the massive headboard that resembled a sleigh. Recognition hit and Jenna bolted upright.

How did she get to Aidan's room? For that matter, how did she get back to the house? The last thing she recalled was dawn illuminating the sky and being too exhausted to walk.

A memory of Aidan carrying her through the woods, cradling her against his powerful chest, exploded in her mind.

How humiliating!

Jenna fell back onto the bed. Geez, one night with him and she'd become a swooning heroine from a romance novel. She snorted and shook her head at how pathetic she'd been, then sat up once more. Jenna knew she couldn't stay in Aidan's room, eventually either he'd return or someone else would find her there.

She threw the covers back and slipped off the bed. Jenna listened, but didn't hear the shower running. She glanced toward the patio. The doors to the balcony were closed.

Where was Aidan? And why hadn't he taken her back to her room? Surely it would've been easier than carrying her up the stairs and tucking her into his bed.

Jenna looked around again. Her gaze landed on a piece of paper, sitting on the nightstand. She saw her name written on it and picked it up.

Jenna,

I had a meeting set for early this morning that couldn't be rescheduled. I didn't have the heart to wake you after what I'd put you through last night. There are things I must tell you, but they can wait until you get back from work.

Aidan

Jenna flipped the note over, but there was nothing written on the back. Not exactly the most romantic message, but she hadn't expected it to be. They'd had sex. Amazing sex. Stupendous sex. But sex nonetheless.

Aidan hadn't proposed marriage. He hadn't even suggested that they date. She appreciated the fact that he'd taken the time to drop her a note, but Jenna wasn't going to read too much into the gesture.

She found the pad of paper Aidan had used to scribble the note in the drawer of his bedside table. Jenna composed one of her own and tucked it under the lamp on his side of the bed where he was sure to find it.

Her note wasn't eloquent, but she did tell him how much she'd enjoyed last night. Jenna hoped that when she saw Aidan again that it wouldn't be too awkward, but she couldn't worry about that now because she had to get to work.

Jenna poked her head into the hall to make sure it was clear, then dashed out of Aidan's bedroom. She ran down the stairs, praying the whole time that no one saw her.

She wasn't ashamed of what she and Aidan had done, but she'd rather avoid the embarrassment of being caught wearing the same clothes she'd worn the night before.

It took three tries, but Jenna finally found her bedroom. She showered quickly and put on some makeup. She was about to pull on her shirt, when Jenna noticed an odd mark near the crook of her neck. She leaned in to get a better look.

It was a love bite.

Jenna ran her fingers over the spot, recalling the moment it happened. She and Aidan had been completely out of control, going at each other like savage animals, biting, clawing and grunting. Jenna had never been one for rough sex, but with Aidan it had seemed natural.

She'd matched him move for move, kiss for kiss, and shout for shout. He'd brought out a side of her that she hadn't known existed. Now that she did, Jenna couldn't imagine being any other way.

Jenna pressed down on the spot. The area was tender to the touch. She examined it closely.

Teeth marks.

She should've been appalled that she'd let him *brand* her in such a way. After all, they weren't teenagers exchanging hickeys. But for some inexplicable reason, she felt the opposite.

Jenna *liked* seeing Aidan's mark upon her skin. It seemed intimate, personal—oddly territorial. Which of course was ridiculous, since it was just a hickey.

She glanced at the evidence of their lovemaking one last time, then got dressed. Maybe next time around she'd tell Aidan to lay off the biting.

If there was a next time, an insidious little voice whispered.

Jenna knew she couldn't make too many plans. She had no idea how things would unfold with Ethan and the lawsuit she planned to file against him. Until she found out, there was no sense thinking about a future with Aidan.

She flipped off the light and rushed out of the room. Jenna hurried down the hall. She could see the door to Aidan's office was closed as she drew nearer. She debated whether to knock and say goodbye.

The note had said he was in a meeting. Would it still be going on? She didn't want to interrupt something important, though she was tempted.

Jenna wanted to see him, even if it was only for a moment. In the end, she decided that wasn't a good enough reason to disturb him. They could talk when she got back.

She left the house and jogged down to the garage. Her Bug was waiting outside for her with the keys in it. Jenna squealed in delight and climbed into her car.

"I've missed you." She patted the Bug's dashboard and started the engine.

Bernie came out of the garage. "How does she sound?"

"*He* sounds great." She laughed. "Please thank Nic for me."

"Will do." Bernie reached into the pocket of his coveralls and pulled out a business card. "Give us a call, if you have any problems."

Jenna took the card. "I will. See you later."

He smiled as she cranked the radio and slipped the car into gear.

Jenna waved to him, then drove off. This time when she turned left toward Breakbend, she knew her life had finally taken a turn for the better.

* * * * *

Robert breathed through his mouth so he wouldn't have to smell her. Jenna's human scent covered Aidan like cheap cologne, making him gag.

How could the Alpha have slept with her without vomiting during the act? The odor was so bad that Robert could almost *taste* her.

He dry-heaved at the thought.

Now that Aidan had slummed it by fucking the human, was it too much to hope that she was finally out of his system and would soon be out of the house?

"Go to my room and grab the file sitting on the dresser," Aidan said.

Robert slipped out of the office and gasped, filling his lungs for the first time in over an hour. He took several deep breaths as he climbed the stairs, trying to get the rank weedy scent of the human out of his lungs.

It wasn't until Robert reached the top of the stairs that he noticed he could still smell her. The scent should've faded.

Robert frowned and searched the hall, but he was alone. He tilted his head and listened. No retreating footsteps. Obviously breathing through his mouth hadn't worked. The human's stench was more powerful than he'd imagined.

He shook his head in disgust and strode down the hall. When he reached Aidan's bedroom door, Jenna's scent became cloying. Robert stared at the door in confusion, then threw it open.

He took one step inside and fell to his knees. Jenna's scent was everywhere and seemed to permeate everything.

Robert gagged and staggered to his feet. He stared in disbelief at the rumpled sheets on the bed.

Normally only Aidan's side of the bed was disturbed, not both. He glanced at the pillows. There were two distinct impressions.

No! It couldn't be. He had to be mistaken.

The Alpha never spent the night with any female. That privilege was reserved for his bondmate.

Robert rushed forward, shoved his nose in the bed, and sniffed. One side of the sheets smelled of wolf, while the other...

His stomach churned as the truth hit. Jenna had slept here. In the Alpha's bed. All night. Her scent was too strong for it to be otherwise.

Why would Aidan allow such a thing? The bond was sacred to the Moonlight Kin. It was said to be a gift from Freki herself.

Robert quickly searched the room, but the human was nowhere to be found. He was about to leave, when he noticed a piece of paper tucked under the lamp. Robert snatched the sheet off the table and scanned the note.

Cold enveloped him as the words and their implications slowly sank in. Robert crushed the paper and tossed it in the wastebasket, then grabbed the folder that Aidan had requested.

Things were worse than he'd imagined. Robert could no longer stand by and watch the pack disintegrate. He had to act now.

As soon as the meeting ended, Robert intended to confront the interloper. If she refused to leave, then he'd have no choice, but to kill her. And he'd do so, knowing that he acted in the best interest of the pack.

* * * * *

Jenna typed her interview up, while Paul Welling

hovered behind her. He'd been acting like a child on Christmas morning, waiting for the go ahead to open the biggest box under the tree.

She finished the last line and hit send, so that it went straight into Paul's inbox. He raced into his office to make sure the email had arrived, then yelled for Jenna to join him. Paul opened his desk drawer and pulled out a stack of twenties.

"This is just something to tide you over until we sell the article to one of the leading magazines. With any luck, we'll be able to get a bidding war going." He handed her the cash. "There should be a thousand dollars there."

The amount was less than Jenna had hoped, but enough to get the legal process started. She shoved the money into her pocket next to the card Bernie had given her. "Thanks!"

"Take the rest of the week off, but I expect to see you here on Monday," he said.

Jenna didn't answer because she wasn't sure she'd be here come Monday. Much depended on what the attorney she was going to hire suggested that she do next. She left Paul's office feeling like a weight had been lifted off her shoulders.

Molly saw her come out. "Did Paul give you the rest of the week off?"

Jenna nodded.

"Did he tell you that we normally don't work on Fridays?" she asked.

Jenna laughed. "No, he failed to mention it." She looked back at his office. The door was closed. He was probably already on the phone, trying to sell the rights.

"He'll be happy now that he has his interview, but I doubt it gets him out of Breakbend," Molly said. "Newspapers aren't what they used to be. Everyone is reading online. Paul's still living in the past."

It didn't matter to Jenna. There was no one right career path these days. Everybody had to get creative.

"What are you going to do now?" Molly asked.

"I have an appointment with an attorney, then I'm going to head back to the Fortier estate," she said.

Molly grinned. "Any special reason you're going back there?"

Jenna looked away. "None that I care to mention."

Molly giggled. "I knew you were holding out on me about Aidan Fortier."

"I don't know what you're talking about," Jenna said.

"That hickey on your neck says otherwise," Molly teased.

Jenna couldn't stop the smile from spreading across her face. "Have a good weekend."

"I will," Molly said. "But I bet yours is better."

She chuckled, hoping Molly was right. Jenna stepped out onto the sidewalk and took a deep breath. She'd parked the Bug down the street, where it would stay while she visited the attorney's office. He was only a few blocks away and she could do with a walk.

Jenna found the office and spent the next hour explaining her situation. She'd been nervous when she first arrived, but Wilson Bennett had quickly put her mind at ease.

By the time she left, the attorney had accepted the job and he'd already started making phone calls on her behalf.

Jenna strolled down the sidewalk with a smile upon her face. It felt good to finally have someone on her side, fighting on her behalf. She could see her Bug peeking out from behind a red truck up ahead.

She dug into her pocket and pulled out her keys. It was only as Jenna drew nearer that she noticed a man leaning against her car. His long legs stuck out, but the truck obscured the rest of his body.

When Jenna was about twenty feet away, the man stood, giving her a clear view of his face. She felt the blood drain from her as her past came crashing down upon her.

"Darling, I've missed you." Ethan opened his arms wide and approached her like he was going to hug her.

Jenna turned to run to the Gazette and slammed into Carl Rich. She bounced off Carl's chest. He captured her wrist and squeezed, until Jenna whimpered in pain and dropped her car keys. He caught them before they hit the ground.

"That's for kicking me in the balls," he spat, then jerked her around to face Ethan. "I believe you have a date in Vancouver that you can't miss."

The bell on the door of the paper chimed. Jenna glanced back and saw Molly step out with a pink sweater in her hands. She waved when she saw Jenna, then her smile slowly faded.

Jenna tried to warn her away with a pointed gaze, but Molly wasn't taking the hint.

"Thought you'd be long gone by now." Molly glanced at her watch. "If I had a sexy beast waiting for me at home, I wouldn't still be here in town."

"I don't know what you're talking about," Jenna said. *Shut up. Please shut up.* There was a chance that Ethan and Carl didn't know about Aidan. Jenna wanted to keep it that way.

Molly's frown deepened.

Ethan pulled Jenna into his arms and stroked her back. "Smile for your little friend," he whispered. "We wouldn't want anything to happen to her."

He was right. It was better to play along, until she could escape. Ethan had already proven that he'd ruin anyone who crossed him. Jenna didn't think he'd blink an eye at dismantling Molly's family's newspaper business.

Jenna gave Molly a strained smile. "As you can see, I have a lot of friends." She indicated to the men. "Too many to keep track of."

"Here in town?" Molly asked, eyeing Carl and Ethan in bewilderment.

"Yes," Ethan said. "If you don't mind, we'd like to continue this reunion in private." He winked at her. "I'm sure you understand."

Molly didn't say anything, but her disapproval was apparent.

"I'll see you on Monday, Molly." Jenna nudged Ethan to distance him from the woman. She had no idea what he'd do, if given half the chance.

"Yeah, see you then." Molly nodded, then walked back the way she came.

Jenna watched her go. Her smile faltered, but did not fade.

Molly looked confused, when she glanced back.

Jenna waved goodbye.

Molly shrugged, then slipped inside the Gazette building.

"It appears Carl was right. You've found yourself a new friend," Ethan said.

"Molly's not my friend. She's just a co-worker." There was a chance he'd leave her alone, if Ethan believed Jenna really didn't know her. He only liked hurting the people she cared about.

"I'm not talking about Molly," he said. "What's his name again, Carl?" Ethan snapped his fingers.

"Aidan Fortier."

Jenna's blood went cold. Molly hadn't mentioned Aidan by name, so how had Carl found out about him? Aidan had only come to town with her one time.

"I knew it," Jenna said. "You've been following me around Breakbend."

"It's my job." Carl smirked.

"For how long?" she asked.

"Long enough," Carl said.

She looked at Ethan. "Leave Aidan out of it. He doesn't have anything to do with us. With this." She waved her hand between them.

Ethan tilted his head and smiled at her.

A long time ago, she would've thought that expression was cute, but now it made Jenna's skin crawl. She'd seen that same smile on Ethan's face right before he'd thrown the legal documents on the table, showing her that he'd swindled her out of her garage.

"I'd love to leave Fortier out it. I really would." He pressed his hand to his chest, feigning sincerity. "But you ran from me Jenna, which proves that I can't trust you. There's no way for me to know for sure that he isn't helping you."

"I told you he's not."

"Once again, I'm only left with your word." Ethan rubbed his jaw thoughtfully. "I suppose there is a way that you could prove to me that you're telling the truth."

She grit her teeth. "How?"

"Return to Vancouver with me willingly as a show of good faith, then I might consider giving your new *friend* a pass." Ethan paused dramatically. "Of course, you'd have to do everything I asked once we got there, but that's only fair considering what you've put me through."

"For how long?" She braced for his answer.

Ethan's smile widened. "Until I finish closing the deal. Shouldn't take more than three months, once the papers are signed."

Three months?

How was she supposed to explain to Aidan that she'd be gone for three months? The separation would destroy their burgeoning relationship before it ever got a chance to start, which was probably the reason Ethan had suggested it. He wanted to see her in pain. He wanted her to lose everything...again.

Jenna's heart thundered in her chest, threatening cardiac arrest. She knew Ethan well. He'd never honor his word. The fact that he'd even brought Aidan's name up meant that he'd been doing research into his background.

What had he found? Heaven help Aidan, if he'd already spoken to the people in town.

She thought about the wolves, Aidan's unusual living arrangements, his odd behavior, and his obsession with privacy.

If Ethan exploited even one of those things, it could destroy Aidan's reputation.

No doubt he'd pursue them all.

Jenna couldn't let that happen. It was her fault Ethan was here. It was up to her to stop him. "I'll do anything you want," she said. "As long as you leave him alone."

"I had no idea you'd grown so attached, so quickly. You've only been here for what, a week?" Ethan touched one of the loose curls hanging near her face. "Carl had suggested that you were sleeping with the man, but I assured him that you were too frigid to be a whore." His gaze lingered on Aidan's love bite, then he looked at the investigator and shrugged. "Guess I was wrong about that too, Carl. She is a slut."

Jenna jerked her shirt over to cover the spot, then glared at Ethan's flunky.

Carl sneered. "I call them like I see them."

Ethan wound her hair around his finger and yanked hard to get her attention. "You know this changes things, don't you?"

Jenna scowled at her ex. "It changes nothing."

"Beg to differ," Ethan said. "When this whole thing started, it was just between you and me. Now that I know you've been sleeping with Fortier, it makes me wonder how much you have told him."

"We never had sex." Jenna's body shook with rage as she lied through her teeth. "I haven't told Aidan anything about you. Not your name. Not where you're from. Nothing. He has no idea who you are. He doesn't even know that we *dated*." She poured her contempt into the last word. "Hell, he doesn't even know that you exist."

Ethan tsked. "I wish I could believe you, but with your history of lying..."

"I never lied," she ground out. "You on the other hand did nothing but."

"Let's agree to disagree." Ethan led her down the street. Jenna had to jog to keep up with his long strides.

"It's important for people like you to understand that it's not okay to screw with people like me. It sets a bad precedence, if these things go unpunished," he said. "That's why I think I'm going to have to make an example out of your friend. You leave me no choice."

"Then I'm not going with you." Jenna struggled to break free. His punishing grip tightened, leaving finger marks on her arm. She cried out, catching the attention of a few people walking down the sidewalk.

He scowled at her, then smiled at the growing crowd, pouring on the charm. "She's had a little too much to drink." Ethan tipped an imaginary bottle to his lips.

The people's reactions to the news varied. Some still looked concerned, while others appeared disgusted by her behavior.

Ethan lowered his voice. "The more you fight, the worse it's going to be for him."

Jenna stopped struggling. What was the use? He'd won. He always won. She thought she could challenge him. Get back what he'd taken. But seeing Ethan today made her realize that she'd been fooling herself. No matter how hard she worked, Jenna would never have enough resources to go toe-to-toe with him.

Ethan looked at Carl. "Let's finish this conversation on the plane." He put his arm around Jenna's shoulders and led her toward a gray SUV. "Come along, darling. We have a lot to discuss."

* * * * *

CHAPTER FIFTEEN

Robert LaBeouf could not believe what he was seeing. A horn beeped and he jerked the wheel, narrowly avoiding a collision. He'd come to town to confront Jenna, but before he got the chance, he'd accidentally uncovered her treacherous secret.

He watched the man pull Jenna into his arms and hold her close. She didn't try to get away. Instead, Jenna smiled and hugged him back, stopping only long enough to chat with a friend.

Once the woman departed, the man put his arm around Jenna's shoulder and led her down the street. Robert seethed on the Moonlight Kin pack's behalf. Aidan had been duped just like he'd suspected.

By a human no less.

Robert turned the car around and cruised by the loving couple once more. He watched Jenna and the men climb into a gray SUV and head out of town. On the way back to the estate, he spotted her car sitting near a coffee shop.

Why hadn't she taken it?

Maybe she was coming back for it? Or maybe she'd gotten everything she wanted from Aidan and the pack and didn't need it anymore. The thought filled him with righteous fury.

The Alpha had insisted that the vehicle be repaired for her. The pack had dropped what they were working on to accommodate his wishes. Josh had even made a special trip into the city to get the parts. And this was how she showed her gratitude.

The only thing that cooled Robert's anger and kept it from becoming a murderous rage was the knowledge that he'd personally get to inform Aidan that his little human pet had run off with another man. He grinned.

Robert couldn't wait to see the look on the Alpha's face when he found out that he'd been deceived.

* * * * *

"Are you certain?" Aidan asked. "Two men, not one?"

His body trembled with barely contained rage. How could Jenna do this to him after what they'd shared last night? After everything he'd done for her?

His wolf couldn't have been wrong about her, could he?

Thank Freki, he hadn't told the pack yet that he'd marked her as his bondmate. Aidan had planned to do so this weekend. Now it was the last thing they needed to hear, especially if she'd run off with two men like Robert said.

What was he going to do? Aidan didn't think he could live without her.

His wolf demanded that he go after her. Find her. Kill the men that she was with and bring her back.

It was tempting, but not the smartest plan, especially if Jenna chose to go with them. The idea that she'd picked another male over him wounded Aidan in a way he'd never experienced before.

The pain seared his soul, leaving him in agony. It was the kind of open wound that wouldn't heal easily...if ever. She'd rejected him. His claws extended. With sheer force of will,

Aidan forced them back inside. This situation called for logic, not emotion.

What if the men were the ones Jenna was frightened of? The ones she'd been running from? Fear replaced some of his anger.

But why would she go with them, if that were the case? There'd been people out. Enough witnesses around that she could've escaped had she wanted to. And why would she embrace one of them? It didn't make sense.

"Tell me again exactly what you saw," Aidan said.

Robert started from the beginning, repeating the story verbatim. "If you don't believe me, you could ask the woman she was talking to."

"Woman?" Aidan asked. "What woman? Why didn't you mention her before?"

"I didn't think about it until now. Seeing Ms. Dane in another man's arms made me forget everything else."

Aidan winced. He couldn't get the picture of Jenna being held by another man out of his mind. His wolf struggled to break the tenuous grip he had on it.

Like a good little wolf, Robert kept his gaze trained on the floor. "I believe the woman works at the paper with Ms. Dane. They had a short conversation, then I saw her go into the building."

Aidan had hoped that Robert was wrong. He knew the wolf wasn't lying. That had been the first thing he'd checked, when he'd reported the news. He wouldn't have put it past him since Robert hated all humans, but in this instance he was telling the truth.

He ran a hand through his hair and scrubbed it over his face. Aidan shouldn't have let her out of his bed. He should've found a way to keep her in his room, until they got a chance to talk.

Jenna was his mate. Was his period. His mark proved it. Didn't matter whether a human male could recognize such a thing. He knew the truth. Soon Jenna would, too.

"What do you want me to do?" Robert asked.

"Nothing," Aidan growled. The last thing he needed was for Robert to involve himself any further. Jenna was his responsibility. He'd have to be the one to ferret out the truth. Even if that truth turned out to be something Aidan didn't want to hear.

* * * * *

"Father, I was using the plane," Ethan whined and gave the phone a petulant pout.

They'd driven to the small airport where Ethan had parked the jet, but it was gone by the time they got there. It was everything Jenna could do not to laugh at his first world problems.

"I realize it's not mine, but I needed it to get back to Vancouver," he said. "I have very important business to attend to. No, it's not more important than yours. I didn't say that."

Jenna watched Ethan pace back and forth like a caged hyena. The dingy room he and Carl had brought her to didn't strike Jenna as the kind of place Ethan would frequent, much less spend the night in. Its faded mauve comforters, cheap worn out furniture, and tissue thin towels did however suit Carl to a 'T'.

"Fly commercial? Are you serious? Why would I do that, when there's a perfectly good corporate jet available?" Ethan stopped walking. "Yes. I understand. When can I have it back?" He squeezed his cell phone until his knuckles cracked. "No chance of getting the plane any sooner?" He paused. "I see."

Carl sat at the table, flipping through a Breakbend visitor's guide. It appeared like he wasn't paying any attention to Ethan, but Jenna knew better. The beefy investigator was like a sponge. He absorbed everything, noted every detail.

"I'll expect it here Saturday morning." Ethan pressed a button to disconnect the call. "I can't believe this. You're sure this is the last room available."

"Yep," Carl said. "There's a fishing tournament in town. We were lucky that I hadn't checked out yet."

Ethan looked around the room and scowled.

What were they going to do until Saturday? Jenna wondered. She didn't relish the idea of staying in this motel room with them for two nights.

"Why didn't you just bring the paperwork with you?" Jenna asked. "It would've saved us both a lot of time and trouble."

Ethan shoved his phone in his pocket and walked over to where she sat on the edge of the bed. "I'm not buying a fast food restaurant from you. This type of land deal requires several attorneys to be present. I can't just pull random people off the street to be witnesses," he snapped.

"I'm surprised you didn't forge my signature," she said.

He looked at her, his expression inscrutable. "I thought about, but again, it wasn't feasible."

She stood and stretched. "What's going to happen now?"

Ethan glared at her. "Now we wait." His gaze swept the room and his lip curled in disgust. "Carl, go out and get us a pizza. Bring back a bottle of disinfectant while you're at it. Jenna and I need some alone time."

Fear slithered down her spine. What did Ethan mean? Surely he wasn't referring to... She shuddered at the thought. If he touched her, she'd kill him. Jenna couldn't imagine having any man's hands on her other than Aidan's.

It didn't make sense given the short time they'd known each other, but it was the truth.

Carl grunted and left the motel.

"Take a seat." Ethan pointed to the chair Carl had vacated.

Jenna walked across the room and sat down.

"I looked up your friend before I left," he said. "Fortier is an interesting man. His resources are comparable to my own. Is that why you slept with him?"

Jenna blanched. "I never said anything about sleeping with him. You're the one with sex on the brain."

"Perhaps, but I'm not the one with the giant hickey." Ethan stared pointedly at the love bite on her neck.

She reached up and covered the spot with her hand. "That's not from Aidan," Jenna said.

Ethan arched a brow. "Carl hasn't seen you with anyone else."

"Yeah, well, Carl wasn't with me 24/7," she said.

"He didn't need to be." Ethan walked over to his briefcase and pulled out a folder. He tossed the contents onto the table.

The photos were of her and Aidan at the restaurant.

"Is that you?" Ethan asked.

Jenna's jaw clenched. "You know it is."

"Good," he said. "We're in agreement. So if that's you, then who is that?" Ethan pointed at Aidan.

Jenna didn't respond.

Ethan sighed. "You might as well answer me. I already know who it is."

"It's Aidan," she said quietly. "But it's not what it looks like," Jenna added quickly.

"Really?" He sat back in his chair and crossed his arms over his chest. "It looks like a romantic dinner for two."

Jenna shook her head. "It wasn't." She pointed to the small notepad on the table in one of the photos. "That was the night he gave me an exclusive interview for the paper."

Ethan's brows rose to his hairline. "I didn't realize wine was a necessary part of the interview process."

Jenna's mouth snapped shut.

He laughed mirthlessly. "So how long have you been fucking him? And don't lie to me. You never could lie worth a damn."

Jenna shot to her feet. "It's none of your business."

Ethan rose from his seat. He stood so close that they nearly touched noses. "Anything that could possibly jeopardize this land deal *is* my business." He pointed to the photos. "I didn't bring Fortier into this mess. You did. Whatever happens to him is all on you."

Tears prickled Jenna's eyes, but she refused to let Ethan see her cry. She'd already wasted too many tears on the bastard. He was right though. If anything happened to Aidan, it would be her fault.

"I need something to drink." She turned away from his knowing gaze.

"There's water in the tap," he said.

Jenna pulled a face. "I was thinking more like a soda. I'm pretty sure that I saw a vending machine tucked between the buildings."

Ethan stared at her. "You run and I'll make it my personal mission in life to destroy him. You understand?"

She nodded, then walked to the door.

"You have five minutes," he said. "If you're not back by then, I'll make a phone call."

Jenna put her hand on the doorknob.

"And Jenna," he said.

She froze.

"Pick me up a Coke while you're at it." Ethan grinned and tossed her some change.

Jenna picked the change up off the carpet and slipped out the room. He was going to try to destroy Aidan no matter what she said or did. She could see the intent in his eyes. All she'd done was delay the inevitable. She just needed to figure out how to delay it a little longer, so she could warn Aidan.

The motel was laid out in a typical V-shape with all the doors facing the parking lot. There were several cars parked in the lot, mostly pickups that held fishing rods in their back windows.

Light blue paint covered the walls, but did little to hide

the age of the building. Jenna wasn't thirsty. She'd just needed to get away from Ethan, so she could think. Warning Aidan was priority number one. Nothing else mattered.

She reached the vending machine and dug into her pocket to retrieve the change Ethan had given her. Jenna bought a couple of sodas, then slowly walked back toward the room. A door opened to her right and an elderly man stepped in front of her, wearing a fishing hat.

"Excuse me," he said. "I didn't see you there."

Jenna smiled. "No problem." She started to walk off, then stopped abruptly. "Sir, could I use your phone?"

His bushy white brows rose and fell like caterpillars inching across a cracked sidewalk. "What's wrong with the phone in your room?"

"It's out of order," she said. "I don't own one of those fancy cell phones."

He snorted. "Me neither. Though the wife keeps badgering me to pick one up." He swept his hat off and scratched his head. "I suppose it would be okay, but don't stay on long. It's a local call, isn't it?"

Jenna nodded.

"Okay, then." He stepped aside.

Jenna hurried into the room and fished out the card Bernie had given her. She tapped her foot impatiently as she waited for the call to connect. She didn't have much time. Two minutes at the most. "Pick up. Pick up. Come on, Aidan."

"Fortier residence," a voice said.

She recognized Robert's nasal tone immediately. "May I please speak with Aidan?"

"May I ask who's calling?" he asked.

Jenna growled in frustration. He knew who it was. He was just messing with her. "I don't have time for games, Robert," she hissed. "I need to talk to Aidan. It's important."

Silence greeted her.

"Are you still there?" What if he'd hung up on her? What

would she do then?

"I'm sorry, but Mr. Fortier is unavailable. He's made it clear that he has nothing more to say to you," he said.

Jenna recoiled. "What? Why?"

Was that what Aidan planned to tell her tonight? Had he decided sleeping with her was a mistake? It hurt to breathe, but Jenna shoved the pain aside. It didn't matter.

She was a big girl. She had entered that clearing with her eyes wide open. No expectations. No demands. They were both consenting adults.

Jenna had known going in what Aidan wanted, because she'd wanted the same thing. If Aidan had misgivings about last night, then so be it. None of that changed what she needed to do.

"Please, Robert."

"I saw you in town with your *friends*," he said. "You couldn't keep your hands off each other. It was disgusting. If you cared at all about Mr. Fortier, you wouldn't have humiliated him in such a public manner."

Jenna's stomach churned. "You don't know what you're talking about." How could he think that Ethan and Carl were her friends?

"Don't I?" he asked. "Your true colors are showing. Not a surprise, considering you got everything you wanted."

All Jenna wanted was to end this. "Robert, please. I'm begging you. This is an emergency. I need to warn Aidan. It won't take long. I promise."

He snorted. "Your assurances are worthless. I'll relay your concerns to Mr. Fortier. Please do not phone again." Robert disconnected the call.

Jenna stared at the handset in disbelief. She could only imagine what Robert had told Aidan. What he would tell him once he saw him again. Would he even bother to let him know that she'd phoned?

This could not be happening. Jenna put the phone down and walked out of the room.

The elderly man had been quietly waiting outside the door to give her some privacy. "Is everything okay?" Concern softened his aged brown eyes and mellowed his tone.

Jenna shook her head. Nothing was okay. Nothing would ever be okay again. She'd lost Aidan before she'd ever really had him.

Once again, Ethan had cost her what she held dear. And thanks to Robert LaBeouf, she couldn't even warn him that trouble was coming.

"Thank you for allowing me to use your phone."

"Anytime," he said.

Jenna walked back to the motel room and opened the door.

Ethan glanced at his watch. "Cutting it close." He held out his hand.

Jenna placed the sodas on the table, then walked into the bathroom and shut the door. The mark on her neck throbbed. She put her hand over the spot and held it there, as if covering it would somehow keep the memory of Aidan's lips burned into her skin.

The tears she'd been holding back welled in Jenna's eyes. She turned on the water, so Ethan wouldn't hear her cry.

* * * * *

CHAPTER SIXTEEN

Aidan lay in his bed surrounded by Jenna's scent. He hadn't allowed the cleaners to change the sheets. Partly as penance for stupidly marking a human and partly because he couldn't stand the thought of losing any part of her.

He'd declined Robert's offer to send a Werewoman to his room. The idea of touching another female was repulsive to him. Aidan knew he couldn't continue to hide. Eventually, he'd have to tell the pack the truth.

Tomorrow the moon run would begin. He'd planned to formally introduce Jenna to the pack once he'd revealed his secret. Thank Freki he'd intended to tell her in person. It would've been disastrous had he put it in writing, since Jenna had taken the note with her.

Should he have worded the message differently? What could he have said or done to get her to stay? Aidan had been asking himself those questions and many others for the past few hours.

He wasn't one for pretty words. Aidan didn't know how to be anything but direct with people. That included members of the female persuasion.

Perhaps he should've told Jenna how he felt? But how

could he, when Aidan had only recently discovered what she meant to him?

The emotions were too fresh, too raw. He was still trying to come to grips with the fact that a human female had turned his life upside down in less than a week.

Aidan had assumed that Jenna had been equally affected by their sudden joining, but her actions said otherwise.

No matter how many ways he examined the situation, Aidan couldn't understand what made Jenna leave suddenly without saying goodbye. When she'd told him that she planned to betray him, Aidan thought she'd been referring to the interview.

What if she hadn't? What if there'd been more to her story? What if Jenna had been trying to tell him about the men and he'd been too caught up in her scent to listen?

Aidan knew she'd enjoyed their time together. You couldn't fake that kind of passion. He would've known. *His wolf would've known.*

He rolled over and stared at the wall. There were no answers written on it. No advice for what he should do next. His gaze dropped to the wastebasket near his bedside table.

There was a crumpled piece of paper in it. Aidan instantly recognized his personal stationary. Maybe Jenna hadn't taken his note with her after all.

If that were the case, then Aidan would finally have the answer he sought.

With trepidation, he climbed out of bed and picked up the wad of paper. Aidan slowly unfolded the sheet and straightened it. His heart tripped in his chest, when he saw his name written at the top of the page. He flipped the paper over, but there was nothing written on the back. It wasn't the note he'd left for her. This was a new one.

So how did the note end up in the trash? Had Jenna changed her mind after she'd written it?

Aidan brought the note to his nose and sniffed. Fur rippled down his arm and his vision blurred, as a familiar odor greeted him. He crumpled the note in his fist and rushed out of the room.

He grabbed the first wolf he saw by the scruff of the neck and slammed him into the nearest wall. "Where is Robert LaBeouf?" Aidan shook Nic hard enough to rattle his teeth.

"N-not sure, Alpha. I think he's running with the pack tonight."

Robert only attended formal pack gatherings. He never ran with the pack for the sheer joy of it. He considered that kind of thing beneath him. Why the sudden change? "Are you sure?"

"Bernie said that Robert was in a good mood. So good that he felt like going for a run," Nic said. "He only mentioned it to me because it was so unusual and thought I'd get a laugh out of it."

Aidan shoved Nic away. "I want you to find Robert and bring him to me."

Nic hesitated.

"Did I stutter?" Aidan bellowed.

"No, Alpha." Nic stiffened.

"Then go! Now!"

* * * * *

Robert yipped excitedly as he ran through the woods. The pack shouldered past him, but tonight he didn't care. He'd saved his fellow Moonlight Kin from what would surely have been a disaster.

The pack raced on, chasing a small herd of deer. The old and the weak had fallen behind. Soon the wolves would catch them and they'd feast. He leapt over a fallen tree trunk and plowed on.

Robert had no idea why Jenna thought she needed to warn Aidan, but he had no doubt that the Alpha could take care of himself.

The lead wolf caught sight of the deer. It barked once and

the pack split in half, circling around the side of the herd to cut the older and weaker deer off before they could escape. Once a couple of deer were separated from the others, the pack formed a loose circle around them and closed in.

The lead wolf lunged for the deer's back leg and got kicked for his efforts. The wolf whimpered, but dove right back in. This time his firm grip on the deer's shank couldn't be broken. Another wolf leapt, latching onto the animal's neck, ripping its throat out.

The first deer fell, then the other was quickly taken down. Blood flowed, filling the air with its sweet coppery aroma. The wolves moved in to feast. Robert threw his head back and howled. He couldn't remember the last time he'd been this happy.

The pack added their voices, then the wolves each took turns tearing off chunks of flesh. Robert stepped forward after the others finished, his mouth watering in anticipation. He could almost taste the prey's sweet blood. He opened his jaw to take a bite.

Something hard hit him from the side, knocking him away from the carcass. Robert rolled snout over tail, then stumbled to his feet. He growled at his attacker.

Nic snarled back, then bones cracked and reshaped as he shifted to his human form.

Robert watched in confusion, then slowly followed suit. "I waited the appropriate amount of time. It was my turn to eat," he barked.

Nic glanced at the two deer like he'd just noticed them. "This has nothing to do with the hunt. Alpha has sent me to get you. He wants you at the house now."

Robert staggered back. "Why? What's happened?"

Nic shook his head. "It wasn't my place to ask."

Stupid wolf, Robert thought. He would've asked.

"You can go." Robert dismissed the wolf, not bothering to hide his disdain.

Nic didn't move. "He told me to bring you to him."

Robert frowned. "I know where the house is. I don't need an escort."

Nic glared at him. "Let's go." He nodded toward a path in the woods.

Robert's gaze strayed to the wolves around them. They'd all stopped feeding and were now staring at him. "Is this really necessary?" he hissed.

"You'll have to ask the Alpha," Nic said. "I'm just the messenger."

Robert chewed his nails as they walked back to the estate. What in the world could have Aidan so wound up that it couldn't wait until he got back?

Had Jenna phoned again, while he was out? Fear settled in Robert's gut, loosening his bowels. He hadn't done anything wrong. He was only protecting the pack from a bad influence. Surely Aidan knew that and would understand his reasoning.

Dread set in when he saw the lights blazing in the windows and a shadowy figure pacing on the patio. "Alpha," Robert said. "You wanted to see me?"

Aidan growled.

A drop of urine slid down Robert's leg.

"Get in the house," he said, then turned to Nic. "You may go."

* * * * *

Once Robert was safely ensconced in his office, Aidan rounded on him.

"I would've told you that she called," Robert blurted, before Aidan said a single word.

"What?" he asked. Jenna had phoned? When? And where was he?

"That's why you summoned me. Wasn't it?" Robert asked, sounding as confused as Aidan felt.

"No," Aidan said. "I had Nic fetch you for another

reason." He walked over to his desk and picked up the crumpled piece of paper he'd found in his room. Aidan held it out for Robert to see. "Explain," he said through clenched teeth. "Then we'll get to Jenna's phone call."

Robert stared at the wad of paper, showing no sign of recognition.

Aidan tossed it at him. The paper bounced off Robert's chest and landed at his feet. He picked it up and opened it. His color drained as he read the note.

"Can you tell me how that note ended up in my wastepaper basket?" Aidan asked. "I know I didn't put it there."

Robert smoothed the crumpled paper in his hands. "I-I have no idea, Alpha."

"Lie!" Aidan roared. "Your scent was all over it. The only other scents on the sheet were mine and Jenna's."

Robert gulped. "I knew the human was going to betray you. I thought it best to lessen the blow."

Aidan's hands curled into fists. "You had no right to interfere."

Robert trembled under Aidan's fierce gaze. "You slept with her. I smelled her on your sheets." His voice cracked. "She spent the night in your room. That privilege was reserved for your bondmate."

Aidan approached him and slowly circled Robert. "I am aware of the social mores."

Robert looked up, his wolf showing in his eyes. "Then why? Why would you dishonor your future mate?"

Aidan stopped directly in front of him. "I haven't. My future mate was right where she needed to be. In my bed, beside me."

Robert stumbled back, a look of horror upon his face. "You didn't. You couldn't. You're...you're an Elder. She's..."

"My bondmate," Aidan supplied.

"But I saw her in the arms of another," Robert said. "If

she were truly bonded to you, she wouldn't have been able to stand the contact."

Aidan's vision faded to red. Claws slipped from his fingertips and his teeth sharpened into vicious points. "This note and the call you failed to mention, tells me there's more to this story. Where's Jenna now?"

"I don't know." He cowered.

"Where is she?" Aidan stormed. His clawed hand rose, preparing to strike a fatal blow.

Urine flowed down Robert's leg, then spread across the floor, forming a puddle. "I swear. I don't know where she is." Robert's hands trembled as he held them up to ward off an attack. He slowly backed away, splashing urine with each step he took.

Aidan looked down in disgust, then back at his *former* assistant.

Robert stopped. "The last time I saw her, she was leaving town with the men. They could be anywhere by now."

Aidan growled. "You didn't note the number she was calling from?"

He shook his head. "No, I didn't think it was important."

Aidan barked out a laugh. "You didn't think it was important."

"I was only doing what I thought was best—"

"Don't!" Aidan warned. He was sick of hearing Robert's excuses. "You should've followed her and found out who those men were before you passed judgment on her."

What if Jenna was forced to leave? What if she were in trouble? The thought nearly brought Aidan to his knees. He'd promised to protect her, even if that meant protecting her from herself.

Why didn't you come to me?

Robert whimpered, his gaze bobbing from the floor to Aidan and back down again. "She had her hands all over that male, rubbing him. She was betraying you. It was only a matter of time before she betrayed the pack," he said.

"The only person who has betrayed me at every turn is you." Aidan snarled. "Now get out of my sight! I want you off the property by the end of the moon run."

His wolf struggled to break his hold. It wanted to tear Robert to pieces and gnaw on his bones. He should just kill him and get it over with, then he wouldn't have to worry about Robert trying to slip a knife into his back.

"For your sake, you'd better hope that nothing happens to her," Aidan said.

Robert rushed for the door. He hesitated when he reached it and looked back at Aidan. "Alpha, I swear—"

"Leave now, while you still can," Aidan said. His control was hanging by a pin. One tug and his beast would be unleashed. "I've made my decision." Now he had to find Jenna.

* * * * *

CHAPTER SEVENTEEN

Jenna spent a fitful night crammed into the small bathtub. Ethan and Carl had taken the beds. Her only options had been to sleep on the floor or in the tub.

After staring at the cigarette burns and mystery spots, she'd decided the tub gave her the best chance of avoiding a future tetanus shot.

The men had checked on her periodically throughout the night to make sure she hadn't escaped. Unlike Ethan, when Jenna gave her word, she meant it. As long as he left Aidan alone, she'd go with him.

That didn't mean that Jenna wasn't planning on sneaking out and trying to phone him again. She was determined to get a message to Aidan, even if she had to send it via pigeon.

Once the men had showered, Ethan had Carl check the area to make sure no one had raised any alarms. The private investigator returned to the motel in late afternoon to let him know everything was fine. No one was looking for Jenna and her Bug was still parked where she'd left it the day before.

Carl had barely settled into the chair, when Ethan sent him out again. This time for food. Carl grumbled something about 'delivery' under his breath, but did as he was told.

Jenna would've found the situation amusing, if it weren't so depressingly serious.

Ethan's cell phone rang. He glanced at the number and smiled. "Manning," he said in lieu of hello.

Jenna wasn't trying to eavesdrop, but the room wasn't big enough to avoid doing so.

"Yes," Ethan said. "She's here with me now." He pulled the phone away from his ear and looked at it, then brought it back. "Can you hang on a minute?"

She sat on the bed, watching and waiting.

Ethan pressed a button. "Dad?" He paced toward the door and back. "That's fantastic! What time will it arrive? Seven?" He nodded. "We'll be there."

Jenna's heart sank. The plane was going to arrive sooner than anticipated. She was running out of time. She had to make a move now because she might not get another chance later.

Ethan clicked over to his other call. "Good news," he said. "Our flight will land around nine-thirty tonight. No sense in waiting. Meet me at my office at ten-thirty and we'll get everything signed and notarized." He hung up and smiled at her.

"I take it we're leaving early?" she asked.

"Yep, we're getting out of this dump," Ethan said.

"What about Carl?" she asked.

Ethan shrugged. "He has a car. He can drive back."

"I'm going to catch a shower before he returns with the food," she said.

With any luck, she could shimmy out of the bathroom window and go use the elderly man's phone again. Jenna would be back before anyone knew she was gone.

Ethan's eyes hardened. "I thought you showered earlier."

Jenna shook her head. "No hot water. You guys used it all."

"Well hurry up," he said. "Carl will be back any minute."

She walked into the bathroom and locked the door. Jenna

was about to turn the water on, when she heard Ethan talking. Had Carl returned already? Jenna leaned her head against the door and listened.

"Were you able to get me a list of Aidan Fortier's enemies and private holdings? What do you mean he doesn't have any? That's not possible," he said. "You need to look again. I want the information waiting for me when I return tonight."

Jenna cursed under her breath. She thought Ethan would at least wait until they got back to Vancouver, before he made good on his promise.

What was she going to do?

She glanced at the shower. Jenna needed to use the phone, but there was no way Ethan would let her. His cell rang again. She heard him answer, but this time Jenna didn't listen to his conversation. She'd already heard enough.

Jenna turned the water on and maneuvered the curtain around the spray, then wadded up a towel and dropped it into the tub to make it sound like someone was showering.

She stepped on the side of the tub and examined the window. Thick coats of white paint covered the window ledge, but couldn't disguise the pockmarked, rotting wood beneath. The size of the window made it clear it had been added for ventilation only.

This was going to be tight.

Jenna slipped the lock, then put both hands on the frame. The window creaked loudly, as she pushed and shoved forcing it to open. She heard Ethan say 'hang on a minute', then he was outside the door.

"What are you doing in there?" he asked. The doorknob twisted, but the lock held.

Jenna manufactured a coughing fit, then flushed the toilet with her foot.

"Are you okay?" Ethan called out.

"I'm fine," she said. "Just had a tickle in the back of my throat. Now can I please have some privacy?"

There was a pause, then Ethan said, "Hurry up. Carl's on the phone. He'll be here in five."

"I'll be out in ten minutes." Jenna looked at the closed door, listening for the sound of retreating footsteps.

The second she was sure that Ethan wasn't hovering outside the bathroom door, she leveraged herself onto the small windowsill.

Broken bottles and discarded cigarette butts littered the ground. It wasn't a far drop, but she doubted that she could land silently. It wasn't like she was a frickin' ninja.

Jenna glanced at the tub. An inch of water sat in the bottom of it. She had to go now. There wasn't much time.

She swung one leg out the window, then squeezed the other through. So far so good. She slid a little further. Her hips caught on the frame, stopping her progress. Jenna wiggled and shimmied, scraping her sides as she contorted her body.

The rotting wood cracked under her weight and crumbled to the ground. She held her breath, expecting to hear Ethan at the door. Jenna coughed again, which was hard to do while balancing on her belly.

"Get your ass out here," Ethan said.

"Can I finish going to the toilet first?" Jenna snapped. "It's that time of the month."

The conversation died instantly like she'd anticipated. No guy liked to discuss that particular subject.

Jenna dropped onto the ground, somehow missing all the glass. The gravel crunched beneath her feet, but she doubted that Ethan could hear her over the shower spray.

She sprinted down the back of the building and around the corner. Jenna came to a halt a few feet from the soda machine.

She peeked around the corner. Carl was coming down the sidewalk toward her. Crap! That was quick. She thought she'd have more time before they discovered that she was missing.

Jenna ducked behind the building and searched for a place to hide. There was none. Her heart trampled her ribs, as she waited for Carl to come around the corner and find her.

She heard change jingle, then drop into the soda machine. A second later there was a loud thud as a soda fell into the tray. Carl repeated the process one more time. Jenna listened to his footsteps fade and heard a door close.

She waited a breath, then glanced around the corner again. Carl was gone. Jenna hurried to the old man's room and knocked on the door. It seemed like it took forever for him to answer. When he did, Jenna rushed inside.

"I'm sorry. I don't mean to be rude, but can I please use your phone again?"

The old man frowned. "You want to tell me what's really going on here?"

Jenna gave him a pleading look. "I can't. The less you know, the better."

"If you're in trouble," he said, "we could call the police."

Jenna held up her hands. "No! No police. They wouldn't be able to help." She dropped her arms. "I just need to use your phone again."

"Be my guest." He pointed to the table.

"Thank you." Jenna picked up the receiver. There wasn't a dial tone. She pressed a couple of buttons, but nothing happened. "Was it working earlier?"

The man shrugged. "Don't rightly know. I haven't tried to use it."

Jenna slumped into the chair by the window and scrubbed a hand over her face. This couldn't be happening. No one had this bad of luck. *No one but her.*

Ethan had won. He'd get the land, ruin her, and take Aidan down while he was at it. The thought of Aidan getting hurt sent a fresh wave of pain crashing down upon her.

He doesn't want to speak to you. Robert had made that clear. There'd been no room for misinterpretation.

The elderly man put his hand on her shoulder and gently squeezed. "Are you sure there isn't anything I can do for you?"

Jenna looked up. She was out of options. Well all but one. And she didn't hold out a lot of hope that it would work. She stood.

"Is there any way that you can give me a ride into town?"

The man nodded. "I could do that."

"We'd have to go now." She glanced out the window. "Right now."

Ethan had her keys, but she was a mechanic. Any mechanic worth their salt could hotwire a car, if they had the right tools.

"Where's your vehicle?" she asked.

He pointed to a faded blue Chevy truck parked outside the door.

"Ready?"

He nodded.

Jenna checked one more time to make sure the coast was clear, then ran for the man's truck. She climbed in a second before the door to Carl's room flew open.

Ethan and Carl rushed out, their heads swiveling left and right as they searched for her.

Jenna dove for the floor of the truck. Had they seen her? Were they coming?

The old man climbed into the driver's seat and looked at her. "I take it you're hiding from those men?"

She nodded.

His brown eyes narrowed. "You haven't done anything illegal have you?"

Jenna laughed. She couldn't help it. The stress was too much. "No. Nothing illegal. Cross my heart." She made the sign of an 'X' over her chest.

The old man chuckled. "I believe you." He reversed out of the parking space, then threw the truck into gear. He gave Ethan and Carl a friendly wave as he drove by.

"What are they doing?" Jenna asked, afraid to move from her spot.

"They just ran behind the building. No doubt they'll be climbing into their vehicle in no time to look for you." His gaze focused on the road. "Where to now?"

Jenna inched up until she could peek out the window. There was no sign of Carl or Ethan, but he was right, they would be coming. "I need to get to Main Street, before they do."

"You got it." The old man put his foot on the gas and the truck shot down the road.

She smiled at him. "Thanks," she said, then added, "I'm Jenna."

"Pete." He shook her hand. "Nice to meet you."

"Pete, you wouldn't happen to have a pair of pliers I could borrow, would you?"

He pointed to the glove box. Jenna reached in and grabbed them. "Perfect," she said. "Thanks!"

* * * * *

Pete dropped Jenna off near her car. She'd spent most of the ride into town constantly looking over her shoulder. She knew she didn't have long. Jenna broke the driver's side window out, not caring that people were watching her.

"It's my car," she said, when someone reached for their cell phone.

They scowled at her and walked on.

Jenna quickly hotwired the Bug and threw it into gear. She pulled a U-turn, cutting off several vehicles. They honked at her, but Jenna didn't care. She hit the gas and the Bug raced out of town. She had to get to Aidan before Ethan did.

* * * * *

"I told you that she was wily," Carl said. "The girl must be some kind of contortionist. You sure she wasn't in the circus before you met her?"

"Positive." Ethan glared at him. "We cannot let her get away."

Carl met his gaze.

"She couldn't have gone far." Ethan pulled a set of keys out of his briefcase and jangled them in front of Carl's face. "I still have these. Even if she hitchhikes back to town, she isn't going to go anywhere."

Carl scratched his head. "What if she went in the opposite direction to throw us off?"

Ethan shook his head. "No, she's heading to Fortier's house. I know it. Jenna thinks she'll be safe there." He rolled down the window and scanned the sides of the road to make sure she wasn't hiding in the tree-line. "I'm sure that Fortier will see it my way, once we have a man-to-man chat. He'll understand why harboring her is a bad idea."

Carl looked in the rearview mirror. "I wouldn't be too sure," he muttered. "He seemed awful possessive, when I saw them together."

Ethan waved his concern away. "I'm sure we'll be able to reach a mutually beneficial financial arrangement."

"Money can't buy everything." Carl glanced in the side mirror, then changed lanes.

Ethan looked at him. "Yes, it can. You just need to have enough of it."

* * * * *

Chapter Eighteen

Jenna spotted the headlights in the distance, when she was a few hundred yards from Aidan's driveway. The Bug was going as fast as it could, but it was no match for the turbo-charged SUV following her.

She slowed just enough to make the turn, then floored the vehicle once more. The massive metal gate came into view. Jenna leaned out of her car and hit the buzzer.

No one answered.

She could hear the roar of the SUV's engine as it drew closer. Jenna hit the buzzer again and again. Where was Aidan? It occurred to her that he might not open the gate because she was the one trying to gain entrance.

Jenna slammed her palm onto the buttons and ran it across them all. In her rearview mirror, she saw headlights go by the entrance to the drive, then heard a screech of breaks.

"Please, Aidan. Let me in," Jenna cried. The SUV backed up and stopped, then turned down the driveway.

The speaker crackled. "I told you that Mr. Fortier doesn't want to speak with you," Robert said.

"Damn it, Robert! They're right behind me," she shouted.

There was a growl and a loud squeak, then Jenna heard Aidan's voice come over the intercom system.

"Open the gate."

The gate slid open. Jenna didn't wait for it to open all the way. The second it was wide enough for the Bug to squeeze through, she drove in.

Gravel crunched under the SUV's wide tires as the vehicle bore down upon her. The high-beam headlights illuminated the woods around Jenna, temporarily blinding her.

The gate reversed direction. Jenna gripped the wheel tight, her gaze locked on the SUV. There was no way she could outrun the vehicle, if it made it past the gate.

"Shut. Shut. Shut," she chanted under her breath.

It was going to be close. Jenna's heart leapt into her throat, as the vehicle barreled toward her.

The distance between the gate and the wall narrowed. It wasn't going to fit. The SUV fishtailed and skidded to a halt. The gate wouldn't hold Ethan off for long, but at least it bought her a few minutes. Jenna exhaled, then hurried the rest of the way down the driveway.

* * * * *

"What the hell are you doing?" Ethan shouted. "Why didn't you follow her?"

Carl stared at the closed gate. "Not sure if you noticed, but that gate is over a foot thick. It would've crushed our vehicle had I tried to drive through."

Ethan slammed his fists onto the dashboard, then jumped out of the SUV. He could hear the puttering of Jenna's car as she drove away.

He pressed the intercom button and waited for someone to answer. No one did. Ethan pressed all the buttons, then walked over and honked the horn.

A voice came on the line. "May I help you?"

"Yes, I need to speak with Aidan Fortier," he said.

"I'm sorry, but Mr. Fortier is unavailable tonight. You'll have to come back some other time."

Ethan growled. "I can't come back. I have a flight waiting. It's imperative that I speak with him tonight. It's about the woman that you just let in. She's not who you think she is."

There was a pause.

"Name please?"

"Ethan Manning."

"One moment."

Now they were getting somewhere. Ethan waited impatiently. Jenna thought she'd found safety. Thought she could hide from him. She was about to find out that no place was out of his reach.

The intercom crackled. "Are you still there?"

"Yes," Ethan said.

"Mr. Fortier apologizes for the inconvenience, but he will not be able to see you tonight. He's otherwise engaged."

Ethan gripped the sides of the console. "Did you tell him who I was?"

"Yes, sir."

"I demand to speak to him," he shouted.

The connection cut off.

Ethan spun around and jumped back into the SUV, then turned to Carl. "Find me another way in."

* * * * *

Aidan was waiting for her, when she got to the house. His arms were crossed over his chest and his sensual lips were pressed into firm line.

Jenna threw the Bug into park and jumped out. She rushed toward Aidan, stopping a few feet in front of him. "I don't have much time. I came here to warn you." She glanced over her shoulder toward the dark driveway.

Aidan's nostrils flared, but he said nothing.

"The man outside that gate is after me." She hesitated. "And because you helped me, he's after you, too."

He stared at her, his expression unreadable.

Jenna wrung her hands. "I know you said that you didn't want to speak to me. I won't bother you after this, but I had to warn you."

"Who is he to you?" Aidan asked softly.

Jenna sighed and her chin dropped. "My ex."

"Ex what?" he asked. "Husband?"

Her eyes goggled. "No! God no! He's my ex-boyfriend."

His body seemed to ripple in response to her answer.

Jenna wanted to run to him. Throw herself in his arms. It hurt to see Aidan keep his distance from her, but she'd respect his wishes.

"Listen," she said. "There isn't time to explain everything. Suffice to say, Ethan Manning is a very powerful man. He has the resources to hurt you."

There was a spark in his eyes at the mention of Ethan's name.

"I thought I could protect you, if I stayed away," she said. "We had a bargain, but he reneged on our agreement."

"You ran from me." The pain in his voice shredded her composure.

Jenna closed her eyes and took a deep breath. "I didn't run," she said. "I led him away."

Aidan arched a brow. "It looks more like you led him straight to me."

She flinched. "I had no choice, when I couldn't reach you by phone."

"I thought you'd left me," he said.

Jenna blinked in surprise. "I would never...I tried calling to let you know that I had to leave town, but I couldn't get through."

Aidan's jaw hardened. "You were going to leave with him?"

"Temporarily," she said. "The bargain was that I'd go with him as long as he left you alone." Jenna shoved her hands in her pockets. "I know you think I'm stupid for going with him, but you don't understand what type of man Ethan is."

Aidan stepped closer. "No." He shook his head. "You don't understand what type of man *I am*. And neither does he."

Jenna growled in frustration. "You don't get it. Ethan is going to dig into your life and uncover all your secrets." She held up her hand, when Aidan opened his mouth to speak. "Even if all he finds is what I discovered, it will be enough to discredit you and ruin your business relationships. He can take the smallest thing and completely destroy your life. He did it to me. He did it to my friend. He can do it to anyone."

Aidan was powerful, but so was Ethan. He could use his many contacts to bring down Aidan's little empire, even if Aidan didn't think so.

He stared at her.

"Aren't you going to say anything?" Jenna needed him to tell her that everything was going to be all right. That he forgave her for leaving. Anything!

Aidan inhaled and slowly circled her. "You smell like him."

Of all the things he could've said, that was what he went with?

Jenna frowned and sniffed her clothes. "I left my things here. I didn't have any clean clothes with me."

"I don't like that smell on you," Aidan said.

Jenna didn't think she stunk that bad. She had showered last night. Sure, she'd had to put on the same clothes, but it was either that or go naked.

"I think we have a bigger problem right now than my body odor. Ethan has a plane standing by to take us to Vancouver," she said. "He's having someone do an in-depth background check on you as we speak. He's searching for your enemies, so he can turn them into his allies. Now that you know, you can prepare for his next move."

"He won't find any," Aidan said. "None living anyway."

"Yes, well, give him time. He's incredibly persistent." She paused. "Listen, Aidan, I'm really sorry I got you into this mess. It was not my intention."

His sharp gaze searched her face.

"I'll get my things and get out of here." Jenna moved to go around him, but was stopped by Aidan's outstretched hand.

"I'm afraid it's too late for that now," he said.

"Too late for what? Just let me grab my clothes. I know Ethan will leave once I do."

Aidan shook his head. "No one is leaving. The estate is on lockdown."

Jenna stared at him. "Lockdown? Why?"

"The wolves. They're hunting tonight." He pointed to the moon. "It's full."

Okay...

"I'll be safe enough in the car. I'm pretty sure wolves can't open doors," she said, not bothering to hide her exasperation. "Now I need to hurry. There's no way Ethan will leave here without me."

Aidan stepped into her personal space. "There's no way he'll leave here with you."

Before Jenna could respond, he grabbed her and tossed her over his shoulder. She struggled to raise her head. "Aidan, what are you doing? Have you lost your mind?"

He didn't answer. Instead, Aidan carried her into the house.

"You need to put me down. This will only make matters worse."

Aidan climbed the stairs two at a time. He didn't put Jenna down until they reached his bedroom. The second he did, she backed away. "I have to go. If I leave now, I can try to salvage this situation."

He stalked toward her, his amber eyes glowing in the low lighting.

Jenna held up one hand. "Aidan, think about this logically."

"Oh, I am." The words had barely left his lips, when his mouth came down upon hers in a punishing kiss.

Large hands cradled her jaw as he tilted her chin to deepen the embrace. Jenna's head spun, as his lips pulled her under. Aidan's tongue darted into her mouth, igniting an inferno inside of her.

With the last of her strength, she wrenched her head away. "There's no time for this."

"There's *always* time for this." Aidan resumed his sensual assault. He devoured her with his teeth, his tongue, his lips. It was as if he couldn't get enough of her. He came up for air long enough to issue one final order. "Take your clothes off."

In that moment, Jenna knew she was lost.

* * * * *

Aidan's beast rode him hard. He couldn't stand the smell of the men on Jenna's clothes. The only scent that should be upon her was his.

He slowly backed her against the bathroom wall, kissing, tasting, and exploring every inch of her mouth along the way. She was protecting him.

Of all the things she could've confessed that was the last thing he had expected. Her confession sealed Jenna's fate, though she didn't quite know it yet.

Aidan didn't need protecting. All he needed was her.

When her shoulders touched the wall, Aidan lifted her by the waist. Jenna's thighs spread the second her toes left the ground. She automatically wrapped her legs around his hips. Aidan growled and his grip on her tightened.

She was his. *Theirs*. They'd marked her. No man could

take her away from them.

A rending sound filled the silence as Aidan ripped the last of her clothes off and dropped them onto the tile floor. Within seconds, Jenna was naked. Her firm breasts quivered as they were crushed against his chest. Her heat seared his flesh.

"I want you," Aidan murmured. "I thought I lost you." He ground his hips into her soft folds and she whimpered.

"Aidan, we have to stop. Ethan isn't going to wait out there forever. He's desperate. He'll do anything to get to me." Her plea ended on a sigh as he slipped two fingers inside her moist channel.

"He'll have to go through me first." Aidan pulled his fingers out and brought them to his nose. He inhaled.

Jenna smelled of hot-spiced woman mixed with a hint of *wolf*. Aidan smiled to himself, licked the juices off, then plunged his fingers back inside of her.

Her body wept as Aidan drove Jenna higher and higher. "Don't ever leave me again." His voice was barely recognizable.

Aidan held her with one arm and shucked his clothes with the other, then he carried Jenna into the shower. Blindly, he turned the water on, needing to remove the other male's scent and replace it with his own.

The moon called to his beast to reveal himself. Aidan clenched his jaw and hung on to his humanity. He had to keep it together for a little while longer.

His hands were thorough as he lathered her up and rinsed her off. Aidan kissed her the whole time, not wanting to be separated.

The second she smelled like Jenna again, he lifted her up and shoved her back against the tile wall, bracing her with his big body. Without preamble, Aidan entered her.

"Mine!" he shouted, driving himself to the hilt.

Jenna cried out as his hard shaft slid home. Her body bowed, bringing her luscious breasts into view. Aidan leaned down and latched onto her nipple.

He sucked hard, drawing the tender flesh deep, then raked it with his teeth. Jenna sobbed. Her blunt nails dug into this back and she pulled him closer.

He'd almost lost her. Aidan was half out of his mind with rage and relief. His beast demanded that he take, he claim—he mark once more. His body shuddered as the moon commanded that he shift.

"Not yet!" he grit out.

Aidan rocked his hips and thrust hard, lifting her higher. His mouth came down upon hers, swallowing her cries. Jenna writhed against him, then her body convulsed.

She tore her mouth away and gasped. "Yes!" she shouted.

Aidan felt his shaft expand, locked in a velvet vise that he had no wish to escape. His body stiffened, then jerked. He felt his essence spill into her. This was where he belonged. Where Jenna belonged.

His gaze strayed to the mark on her neck. His mark. Aidan felt his teeth lengthen to sharp points. Blood roared in his ears as he licked the spot once, twice, then bit down.

Just like the first time, blood rushed into his mouth, firing his senses. Unlike their first night together, this time Jenna was totally aware of what was happening. Her breath hissed out of her lungs, as his sharp teeth held her in place.

Aidan expected her to fight him, shove his head away, or at least try to resist. Instead, Jenna did something that shocked and humbled him. She reached out and cradled his head, holding him to her body.

Overwhelmed with a tidal wave of emotion, Aidan's knees quivered, threatening to give out. He licked the wound, letting the water wash the blood away.

Jenna had given him the gift of trust. "Thank you," he murmured, nuzzling her neck. Aidan would remember this moment for the rest of his life.

Someone pounded on the door to the bedroom. Whoever it was didn't wait for Aidan to answer. Three of his men rushed into the room. Aidan slipped out of Jenna and pushed her behind him, ready to fight to protect her.

He turned the water off. "What is the meaning of this?" he snarled.

Bernie stepped forward. "The humans have breached the walls. They're inside the compound."

"Find them!" Aidan waited for the men to leave, then turned to Jenna. Her flushed face was now pale with fear. "I need you to wait here. Don't come outside no matter what you see or hear. It's not safe. The wolves will be out in force. When they are hunting, everything in the woods looks like prey."

"I'm not afraid of my wolf," she said.

He gazed down upon her, letting the emotions show that he did not dare speak aloud. "You should be. He's more dangerous now than he's ever been." Aidan kissed her hard, then rushed out the door...naked.

* * * * *

CHAPTER NINETEEN

Wait inside while he goes off to face Ethan on his own. Naked. Not gonna happen.

Jenna wasn't stupid and she wasn't blind. She knew something seriously weird was going on with Aidan. She had no idea what it was, but she was determined to get to the bottom of the mystery just as soon as she saved him and her wolf.

Aidan had implied that he was just as dangerous as Ethan, but she didn't believe him. He'd gone out of his way to protect her. Now it was her turn to protect him.

Jenna quickly gathered her clothes and was about to get dressed, when she caught a glimpse of herself in the mirror.

So that's what it looked like to be ravished. Her gaze was drawn to the mark Aidan had left. The spot was more distinct now that he'd bitten her again. Deep enough to leave a scar.

She'd worry about Aidan's biting fetish later.

Jenna dressed quickly and opened the door. She took one step out the room and walked straight into Nic. She stumbled back.

"Nic?" Flustered by his sudden appearance, she asked,

"What are you doing here?"

He glanced at the love bite on her neck. Nic's eyes widened in surprise, then his gaze dropped to the carpet. "Aidan asked me to look after you."

Jenna's eyes narrowed. "Really? Then why does it look like you're standing guard?"

Nic had the good grace to blush. "Standing guard is a form of looking after you."

"Funny," she deadpanned. "Now get out of the way. I have to stop Aidan."

Nic didn't budge.

"Seriously, big guy, I need you to move. Carl is armed." The words had no sooner left her mouth, when four shots rang out.

Nic jolted.

Jenna gasped, then shoved him out of the way.

"Wait!" he shouted. "Jenna, come back!"

She didn't look to see if he was following. Jenna kept running. She ran to the front door, then switched course at the last second. Nic cursed and slammed into the door, his size preventing him from easily changing direction.

Jenna sprinted for her room. She made it inside and locked the door. Nic pounded on the wood, demanding entrance.

She had no time to waste. Jenna bolted across the room and threw open the patio door. She could hear the wolves howling, the mournful sound ripping at her heart.

Had Carl shot at Aidan and his men or had he fired at the pack? What if they were hurt? Cold seeped into her bones until they ached. They had to be okay. For her there was no other option.

Jenna ran into the woods, stumbling over fallen tree limbs and crashing through bushes. She heard Nic behind her. He was gaining ground. He should've caught her by now, but for some reason he'd let her escape.

The sound of the howling grew louder. Jenna's eyes

finally adjusted to the full moon's glow. She could see a clearing up ahead and shadows moving.

Jenna broke through the tree-line. There were two wolves lying on the ground, whimpering and crying. A dark stain spread rapidly beneath their bodies.

Carl brandished his pistol, swinging the gun wildly, threatening to shoot the next animal that moved. He aimed at a big, black wolf, standing in the middle of the pack.

Jenna recognized the animal instantly.

It was *her wolf.*

"No!" Jenna screamed and raced forward. She jumped in front of the wolf, before Carl could fire. "Don't shoot." She held up her hands, knowing that wouldn't stop a bullet.

Carl's hand shook. "Get out of the way. These aren't wolves. They're monsters."

Ethan's pale face registered shock and something else. His gaze darted frantically from wolf to wolf, as if he were waiting for something to happen.

The wolves continued to howl and snarl, baring their fangs. They slowly circled the men, searching for a weakness so they could attack.

"You shouldn't have shot them," Jenna said. "They weren't bothering anyone."

"Move aside," Carl said. "I can't get a clean shot."

Jenna stepped every time her wolf did, resting her hand on its head, so that Carl would never have a clear line of sight. "Just go!" she pleaded.

"You don't understand." Carl checked his ammunition.

No, she didn't understand what was happening, but right now Jenna didn't care. She just needed to protect her wolf. "Leave now and I'll come with you," she said.

The suggestion seemed to jerk Ethan out of his stupor. He held out his arm and gestured for her to come to him.

Jenna shook her head. "Not until Carl lowers his weapon."

"Do it!" Ethan shouted.

"But, boss," Carl said.

"I said do it!"

Carl lowered the gun barrel.

"He's put it down. Now come here," Ethan said.

Jenna took one step and Ethan lunged for her. He grabbed her around the throat and pulled her against his chest.

"What are you doing?" Jenna gasped. She tried to wiggle out of his hold, but it was impossible. He had a death grip on her.

Ethan's gaze remained locked on her wolf. "I'm not leaving here without her." He tightened his grip until she could barely breathe.

Jenna choked. "Who are you talking to?"

"Him." He pointed to her wolf.

"Are you insane? That's an animal," she said.

He shook his head vehemently. "No, it's not."

The black wolf's form shimmered like waves of heat rising from asphalt. Fur receded and disappeared. The process only took a few seconds. When it was over, Aidan stood naked in the clearing.

Jenna couldn't believe what her mind was telling her. It was like the film had snapped inside her brain. She knew what she'd seen, but the knowledge did not compute.

Magic wasn't real and werewolves didn't exist. Everyone knew that, even children, but she was all out of rational explanations.

"Jenna's not going anywhere," Aidan said. "Not with you. Not with him." His amber eyes glowed in the dark, reflecting the moonlight. "She's mine."

"It was you," she whispered. "All along."

He nodded, but his gaze never left the men.

"How?" she asked. "How is any of this possible?" It couldn't be. Jenna had to be suffering from a head injury. She was probably lying in a hospital right now. That was the only thing that made sense. Or it would, if Ethan's hand around her throat didn't feel so real.

Aidan didn't answer.

"Jenna's coming with me," Ethan said. "We have business that doesn't involve you."

Aidan stepped forward and the wolves fanned out. "If it involves her, then it involves me."

She shook her head. "Aidan, back away. I don't want anyone else to get hurt because of me."

"Not going to happen," he said. "You don't understand what you mean to me. What you mean to my people." His tone told her that he wasn't bluffing.

Jenna watched the wolves as they prepared to attack. "Ethan, let me go or you're going to die."

He shook his head and held her tighter. "Uh-uh, I'm going to expose your freak boyfriend and his friends." He indicated to the pack.

"That's unlikely given who your family is," Aidan said. "Their reputation has been carefully cultivated over the years. They're not about to let you or anyone else destroy what they've worked so hard to obtain."

"Carl's my witness," Ethan said.

Aidan gave him a sad smile. "It's my job to protect the pack from any and all threats."

"I knew you were a piece of trash, Jenna, but I didn't think you would sink so low that you'd actually fuck an animal." Ethan gestured to Aidan.

Aidan flinched and couldn't meet her gaze.

"Now we're getting out of here." Ethan took a step back. "Shoot him if he moves."

"No!" Jenna cried.

"I'm invoking Lycanian law," Aidan said. "Acknowledge if you accept my ruling."

The wolves began to howl.

Aidan's gaze moved from Ethan to Carl. He seemed unnaturally calm. "You are both a threat to the pack. This cannot be allowed."

Carl inched back, glancing over his shoulder, searching

for a means of escape.

"Shoot him, damn it!" Ethan bellowed.

Carl raised the pistol and took aim.

Aidan gave an almost imperceptible nod.

Wolves leapt from the shadows, landing on Carl, ripping his gun out of his hand. They tore into his flesh, shredding skin and breaking bone in seconds. By the time they were finished, all that was left of the private detective was a pile of bloody clothes and a gold ring that had been on his pinky.

Aidan stared dispassionately at the macabre scene, then slowly looked at Ethan. "You now have a choice to make. You can let her go and leave this place never to return or you can join your friend in death."

"P-people are going to know what you've done," Ethan stammered.

Aidan took a step closer. "And what exactly are you going to tell them? That werewolves ate your hired hand?"

Ethan's mouth opened and closed as the reality of the situation hit him. His gaze pleaded with hers.

Jenna almost felt sorry for him. Almost. Her stomach churned as she stared at Carl's remains. It didn't have to end like this. They could've just left.

The nausea soon gave way to...*hunger*. Jenna's eyes widened, when her mouth started to water. She clutched her stomach.

"It's okay," Aidan said, looking directly at her for the first time.

But it wasn't okay. There was something seriously wrong with her.

"Make your decision, but know this before you do," Aidan said. "My wolves are everywhere—that includes your precious Vancouver. If you do anything to harm the pack or if you come after Jenna again, they will find you and they will do the same thing to you that they just did to that man."

The wolves snapped at his heels. Ethan tried to use Jenna as a human shield, but there were too many of them.

"I'll have your answer now, human."

Ethan looked at Jenna one last time, then shoved her away. Aidan caught her before she fell. Ethan didn't hesitate. He turned and ran into the woods.

"Follow him," Aidan said.

Several wolves peeled off from the pack and ran into the woods after him.

"Summon Gabe to tend to the injured."

* * * * *

Aidan was afraid to look at Jenna. Her green eyes had been so wide, she'd looked like a Manga character. He'd smelled her fear, but he couldn't do anything about it. She had to know the truth. The whole truth. In his gut, Aidan believed she was strong enough to handle it and what was to come.

He guided her through the woods back to the house. Aidan didn't touch her. She looked like she'd shatter if he did. Her teeth were chattering and sweat covered her skin.

"What's happening to me?" she asked without looking at him.

Aidan didn't answer. Instead, he walked her into the house and back to his bedroom. The second he closed the door Jenna began to pace.

"I'm the same man you had dinner with," he said. "The same one you made love to. I'm not an animal. Not in the way that he implied."

She glanced at him, but didn't stop moving. "My skin itches. It feels like bugs are crawling beneath it."

Aidan moved away from her, giving her some space. "I know this is a lot to take in."

Jenna stopped and glared at him. "You think? I just saw a man ripped into pieces by...by... What are you exactly?"

He sighed. "My people have had many names throughout the centuries, but we are called the Moonlight Kin." Aidan shrugged. "Humans have another name for us."

"Werewolves," she whispered. "The people in town were right."

Aidan nodded.

"But how? Werewolves don't exist." She started pacing again. "How could you have remained hidden without anyone finding out?"

"It's getting harder and harder to do with the technological changes, but we manage."

"I know you're telling the truth because I saw it with my own eyes, but the whole thing is preposterous. Are you sure I'm not lying in a hospital somewhere hooked up to tubes?"

"I assure you this is real," he said.

She stopped walking and stared at him again. "You bit me." Jenna placed her hand over his mark. "I thought it was just a weird fetish, but it's not. Is it?"

Aidan wasn't ready to discuss what the bite meant yet. Not until he had a better idea of how she was going to react. "Do you plan to return to Vancouver?"

The change of subject surprised her. She seemed to think about it a moment. "Getting my garage back was all I've been dreaming about for the last few months. Now, I'm not sure I want it anymore." Jenna crossed her arms over her chest. "Vancouver holds too many bad memories for me. Besides, what I've seen tonight isn't exactly something I can ever forget."

"No," he said. "This night will stay with you for the rest of your life."

She shivered. "What happens now?"

Aidan arched a brow. "That's entirely up to you."

"Would you really let me leave?" she asked. "I know your secret."

He stared at her a long time, trying to figure out how to answer. She did know his secret, but not all the secrets he'd kept. "You are not a prisoner, Jenna. I won't force you to stay." He might beg her to, but only as a last resort.

She bit her lip. "Good to know." Jenna started moving again. "Hypothetically, what would happen if I stayed?" she asked, then added, "Do you even want me to stay?"

"You already know the answer to that question," he said, feeling a glimmer of hope.

She took a tentative step closer. "Okay, then answer my other question."

"What do you want me to say?" he asked.

"I'm not like you, so how would it work?" She ran her hand along her arm to ward off a chill.

Aidan closed the distance between them. "Would you like to be?"

Jenna balked. "What are you going to do, raise a magic wand and presto-chango I'm instantly like you?"

"You watch too many movies." Aidan shook his head.

She sighed. "Maybe, but that doesn't change the facts of the situation. I'm not like you."

He brushed his fingertips along her jaw. "You could be, but once the process is done, it cannot be reversed."

"Would I be like you then? Like the others?" Her sharp teeth latched onto his thumb.

"Yes." Aidan smiled encouragingly. "You'd be part of the pack, part of the family—a very important part."

* * * * *

Everything was happening too quickly for her. Jenna knew she should slow down, but it felt like her blood was boiling in her veins and for once it wasn't because she was standing close to Aidan.

This was crazy. Insane. Any normal human being would run screaming from the house, but Jenna had never been typical. Nothing about her life had ever been normal. Aidan was offering her a chance to have a family. A real family for once in her life. Could she really pass that up?

She couldn't deny her feelings for the man. If she'd been

in doubt, that ended when she thought Carl was about to shoot her wolf. Panic had overcome her.

In that moment, Jenna had felt such a profound sense of loss. It hadn't made sense at the time, but now she knew why. When she'd seen Aidan shift for the first time, all she'd known was relief.

"What would I have to do?" she asked nervously.

"Nothing." He shook his head and kissed her. "It's already begun."

Jenna's eyes widened. "The bite."

He nodded. "The bite."

"I thought that was a myth," she said.

He shrugged. "Some things have a grain of truth."

"You could've asked before you made that call, since it's my life we're talking about. I would've liked to have been consulted first," she said.

"I understand," Aidan said. "But it was out of my hands. The wolf had chosen its mate."

"My wolf?"

He smiled. "Your wolf."

"Will it hurt?" Jenna swallowed hard.

"A little," Aidan said. "But I'll make sure that all you remember from the change is the pleasure." He pulled her into his arms and kissed her, then made good on his promise.

* * * * *

EPILOGUE

Two months later...

Jenna took off through the woods, jumping over tree roots and racing around bushes. She could hear Aidan behind her, his panting breaths getting closer. He jumped out from behind a tree trunk.

She yipped and dodged right, slipping easily under a downed limb. Aidan barked and followed her. They raced through the woods, enjoying the pleasure of the night.

It had taken Jenna a while to get the hang of the change. She hadn't quite gotten to the point where she could control it, but she'd finally recognized when it was about to happen.

Aidan herded her toward his favorite spot. Jenna let him. It was a game they played that they both enjoyed. He shifted when he reached the small pool of water. Jenna did the same.

"That was fun. Let's do it again." She grinned at him.

"Soon." He brushed his lips over hers, stealing a kiss. His big hands slid down her body, resting on her shoulders.

Jenna sunk into the embrace, enjoying the sensual exchange.

Aidan's grip firmed and he...pushed her into the pool. Jenna came up sputtering and gasping. Gooseflesh rose over her skin from the cold water.

"Oh, you're in trouble now, mister." Her teeth started to chatter. "I can't believe you did that."

Aidan laughed. "I told you I'd pay you back when you least expected it."

Jenna bit her lip to keep from smiling. "Are you going to help me out of here?"

"And have you pull me in? I think not."

"Spoilsport." She laughed.

Aidan's head jerked to the right. "Don't move!" He growled and his body started to shimmer and shift.

The foliage parted and a huge behemoth of a man stepped into the small clearing. He stood a good four inches taller than Aidan and his shoulders were nearly a foot wider. His face was *Elfishly* pretty, but he had the body of a professional wrestler.

If you could get past the fear factor, he might be kind of cute. Though Jenna would never say so in front of Aidan.

The man had long white hair and silver eyes that moved like mercury. Jenna ducked down, until her head and chin were the only things visible.

Aidan stopped mid-shift. "Tristan? What are you doing here?"

"I've been sent by the Lycanian Elders to check on you and your new mate. A complaint has been filed." His shimmering gaze flowed from Aidan to Jenna.

"Let me guess, Robert LaBeouf?"

Tristan flashed teeth, but he didn't smile. Jenna had a feeling he rarely smiled.

"You know I cannot tell you who has filed the complaint," Tristan said. "Not until I've finished with my investigation." He took a step toward the pool, but Aidan cut him off with a deep growl.

"What exactly are you investigating?" His voice remained calm, but his body was tense.

"You are the second among us in the last several months

who has chosen a human for a mate," Tristan said. "It has raised some concerns. We need to determine whether the anomaly is contained within your bloodline or if outside forces are at work."

Aidan stiffened. "Those concerns have not been brought to me. Odd, since I am still an Elder."

Tristan arched a snowy white brow. "For now."

"And if it's not my bloodline?" Aidan asked.

"There are others who do not care for our kind," Tristan said. "As an Elder, you know this."

Aidan paled. "The *Darkling* have not entered this realm for centuries."

"Yet, I've found signs that indicate otherwise." Tristan moved to go around Aidan, but he stopped him again.

"I will not harm her," Tristan said. "I swear on my family honor."

This time when he stepped to the side, Aidan didn't try to hinder his progress.

"I am Tristan Chevalier." He crouched down next to the pool.

Jenna ducked down even further. "Nice to meet you." She didn't extend her hand for fear she'd flash him. She hadn't gotten used to how at ease the wolves were with their nakedness.

Tristan smiled. "She smells like you." He sniffed. "So does the pup she's carrying."

Jenna's eyes widened. They hadn't told anyone yet. They were waiting, enjoying the moment for themselves.

"What are the *Darkling*?" Jenna asked.

"They are the stuff of nightmares." Tristan rose. "I will let the Elders know that your bond is intact and that you've bred true."

Aidan stared at him. "You do that." Sarcasm dripped from his words.

"Keep your eyes open," Tristan said. "If the *Darkling* are back, then we'll need all the strength we can muster."

"I will," Aidan said, glancing at Jenna with concern. "If they have returned, they will seek the Sighted Ones."

"I know." Tristan stepped into the woods. "It's why I intend to find them first."

Before he could disappear, Aidan stopped him. "Once the wolf makes its decision, there's nothing you can do to change its mind."

Tristan looked at him, his expression solemn. "I won't have to worry about that."

Aidan grinned. "Funny," he said. "I thought the same thing."

Tristan trembled like someone had walked over his grave, then his image wavered. A second later, a white wolf the size of a polar bear stood in his place.

He stared at Aidan with those fathomless silvery eyes for a moment longer, then silently raced into the woods.

Jenna struggled out of the pool of water. Gooseflesh covered her skin. Shivering, she asked, "Should I be worried?"

Aidan pulled her into his arms and held her close, then kissed her forehead. "No, Tristan's just being cautious. It's his nature. *Our nature.*"

She snuggled against his chest. "I get that, but what about the rest of it? The whole human-wolf, wolf-human thing?"

"Ah, that." Aidan laughed. "Tristan thinks he can outrun fate."

"If that were the case, then I wouldn't be the Alpha's mate." Jenna playfully nudged him in the ribs.

"No." He nuzzled her ear. "But you'd still be Aidan's mate."

# # #

If you enjoyed this book, please consider **LENDING IT** to a friend. If you really loved Aidan and Jenna's story, then please consider leaving a **REVIEW**.

For more information about Jordan's upcoming books, sign up now for her newsletter:

http://www.JordanSummers.com/contact/

OTHER BOOKS BY JORDAN SUMMERS

Dead World Prequel:
Raphael
Dead World Prequel:
Kane
Dead World 1: Red
Dead World 2: Scarlet
Dead World 3: Crimson

Moonlight Kin 1:
A Wolf's Tale
Moonlight Kin 2:
Aidan's Mate
Moonlight Kin 3: Nic
Moonlight Kin 4: Tristan
- Coming Soon

Phantom Warriors 1:
Bacchus
Phantom Warriors 2:
Saber-tooth
Phantom Warriors 3:
Talon
Phantom Warriors 4:
Arctos
Phantom Warriors 5: Linx
Phantom Warriors 6: Riot
Phantom Warriors
Anthology Volume 1
Phantom Warriors
Anthology Volume 2

Atlantean's Quest 1:
The Arrival
Atlantean's Quest 2:
Exodus
Atlantean's Quest 3:
Redemption
Atlantean Heat 3.5
Atlantean's Quest 4:
The Return
Atlantean's Quest 5:
The Dark King
Atlantean's Quest Bundle
Volume 1
Atlantean's Quest Bundle
Volume 2

Tears of Amun
Heat of the Night
Gothic Passions
Rose's Rapture
Paris After Dark

Ghost Hunter: Solomon's
Seals

Private Investigations
Mesmerized
Hot Shot
Ride Em' Cowboy
Off Limits

MOONLIGHT KIN 3: NIC
UNEDITED EXCERPT

Gravel crunched under Nic La Croix's truck tires as he turned onto the long driveway. Trees and dense underbrush lined the road, leading him deeper into the woods. He ran his hand through his shaggy hair and the tension in his muscles released as wilderness surrounded him.

Nic didn't have long to enjoy the feeling. The tightness came right back as a steady thump, thump, thump reached his ears. So much for convening with nature. After a quarter-mile, the trees parted to reveal a crude gravel parking lot.

On the far side of the lot, a large wooden structure squatted like a toad against the tree-line. The roof slanted to the left and looked to be under imminent threat of collapse. Chipped red paint covered the front of the building, while ignoring the sides. The splash of color did little to disguise the building's deteriorated condition.

A flashing pink neon sign hung above the entrance to the bar. The first "T" and the last "S" of its name were burned out. Instead of spelling "Sticks", the sign now read "Sick."

The new name is more fitting for the shifter bar, Nic thought.

He stared at the crowded lot, debating whether to leave. The only parking spots left bordered the trees and were nowhere near the entrance. Not that it was a problem. The position would make it easier to get out when the time came. Nic looked at his watch. Not yet six o'clock and already packed. It would only get worse.

After a hard day's work, he wanted a beer, but Nic wasn't sure fighting the crowd would be worth it this close to the full moon. He glanced up at the sky. The sun hadn't set yet and the moon was already rising. Its pregnant appearance made all wolves anxious, but was especially difficult for the younger ones, who thought they had something to prove.

Restlessness snaked its way through Nic's body, leaving him edgy. The feeling was happening more and more lately, but had nothing to do with the moon and everything to do with not being bondmated.

Nic listened to the steady beat of the music and heard a crowd roar. The sound quickly morphed into howls. Blood simmered in his veins as he fought the urge to join in.

It had been two months since he'd moved off Aidan Fortier's estate and away from the pack. Two months since he'd sworn off fickle human females.

He'd always fallen too hard and too fast for his own good. It had gotten him hurt on more than one occasion, but this time had been the worst because he'd fallen for his Alpha's mate.

Nic couldn't bear to be around Aidan's mate, Jenna Dane, feeling the way he felt about her. Every day he watched her belly ripen with Aidan's child, and he couldn't help thinking what if...

It didn't matter that it was the man in him that wanted her, not the wolf. Pain was pain.

Next month Jenna would give birth—thanks to shifters' short gestation periods. Pregnancy wouldn't be possible if she wasn't truly Aidan's bondmate, but seeing her expectant, glowing, and happy only compounded his loneliness.

Maybe someday he'd get used to sleeping alone, but Nic had his doubts.

Once a pack animal, always a pack animal.

Being homesick for his pack was why he found himself at Sticks and not home at the little house he'd rented outside of town. The desire for a beer and to be around his own kind was a temptation he couldn't resist. Nic drove to the tree line and threw the truck into park, then climbed out. One beer, then he'd leave. Okay, maybe one and a half. It would take a lot more than that to impair a Were.

The music pumped hard, vibrating his chest as he strode toward the bar. There wasn't a cover charge for shifters, only humans. Not that many humans came out to this place or even knew about it. And the ones that did, knew the score going in.

Weres had groupies, just like rock bands. Their animalistic, insatiable nature drew them from hundreds of miles away. The humans who partied at Sticks came here for one reason and one reason only—to hook up with a shifter.

Nic wasn't looking for company, and he certainly wasn't looking for a fight, but he did want a beer. A nice cold one. For that, he'd put up with the loud music and the boisterous crowd.

"Hey, Derek," Nic said. "How's it going?"

The burly doorman grinned, flashing long canines. "Different day, same shit."

"I hear you. Lucien Bellard working tonight?" Nic asked.

His best friend bartended most nights, but he did get off work on occasion. When that happened, he didn't show up here. He took off for the mountains.

"Yep, he's behind the bar, keeping a close eye on the pups," Derek said. "A bunch of them came in earlier itching to test their claws. Remember when you were that young?"

Nic laughed. "Hell no! I was never that young."

Derek chuckled. "Me neither."

It was common for young Weres to come to Sticks. The

place allowed them to blow off steam and test their skills. Pack life was all about hierarchy. Young wolves were constantly looking for ways to better their positions. Nic didn't have to worry about that anymore. He'd earned his spot in Aidan's west coast pack through blood, brains, and brute strength.

Nic leaned forward and waited for Derek to sniff him. It didn't matter who or what you were, everyone got sniffed on their way into Sticks. It was a surefire way to keep out the troublemakers and to identify the humans. If you weren't pack, you got your hand stamped with a wolf paw. It was an inside joke that only regulars recognized.

"You're good to go." Derek hiked his thumb over his shoulder. "You came on the right night. The band's supposed to be good tonight."

"Probably won't stay that long," Nic said. "Just here for a beer."

The bouncer shrugged, then gave him a look that said "suit yourself."

The inside of the bar was even more crowded than the parking lot. Most of the worn tables were already occupied, and the only stool available sat at the end of the long, polished oak bar. Weres lined the bar three deep. They kicked up sawdust beneath their feet as they waited to get served.

Nic made his way to the end of the bar and scanned the crowd. He didn't think many from Aidan's compound would be there, but it didn't hurt to check. He wouldn't mind shooting the breeze with a familiar face.

A dark head popped up above the crowd. Lucien waved to him, his green eyes glittering mischievously.

Nic nodded in acknowledgment. It had been a while since he and Lucien had had a chance to catch up, but it didn't look like that would change tonight.

Two pups knocked younger Weres aside as they pushed their way to the front of the crowd. Nic didn't recognize them, which didn't mean much since the west coast Moonlight Kin were spread out over several states, but he did recognize the type.

Impatience oozed from their pores. Some pups naturally fell into their pack position. Others fought for purchase. These two fell into the latter camp. Their stance screamed aggression. In a shifter bar, that was a good way to get your ass kicked.

Nic watched dispassionately as they stopped at the bar and waved money in front of Lucien's face. *I wouldn't do that if I were you,* he thought. His best friend didn't have a lot of patience for assholes.

Lucien's lip curled and a growl rumbled out of his wide chest. The Celtic tattoos that started at his neck and encased both arms rippled as he tensed. Smart pups took a step back to give Lucien space. The two with the money in their hands didn't move.

Some pups just had to learn the hard way.

A claw came out and speared the money, yanking the bills from the closest pup's hand. Lucien tossed the money into a tip jar, then yelled, "Next!"

The startled pup opened his mouth to complain, but must've got a look at Lucien's expression and changed his mind.

Nic sighed. He wasn't in the mood to put up with this kind of crap tonight. He turned to leave, but before he could go, a beer slid down the bar and stopped in front of him.

He looked over in time to see Lucien grin, then his friend went back to filling orders. The two pups who'd been flashing money glared at him. Nic raised his pint glass in salute, then took a deep swig. The cold, crisp flavor of hops and barley exploded on his tongue. He leaned his back against the edge of the bar and scanned the crowd.

Several groupies had already snagged a table near the front, close to the band. The location put them in the position to be seen by everyone, which Nic supposed was the point.

The band was still setting up their equipment. He couldn't tell if they were human or not. He spotted a few wolf paw stamps in the crowd, but not many. Nic made a mental note to avoid them and went back to enjoying his beer.

A few minutes later there was a knock on the bar. Nic turned to find Lucien smiling at him.

"You look miserable as ever," Nic said.

His friend had a perpetual smile on his face and took delight in the little things, especially if those things came in the form of aggravating a friend. But there was more to Lucien than that. Every once in a while the mask would slip and Nic would glimpse the darkness he kept hidden from the world.

Nic had never asked what caused the shadows. He figured if Lucien wanted to let him know, he would. Until then, he'd be there whenever his friend needed him and would continue to keep up pretenses.

"You're the one lurking at the end of the bar, my friend. How do you expect to meet anyone with that sour expression on your face?" Lucien asked.

"I don't," Nic said. "I'm just here for the beer and your stellar company."

Lucien laughed. "Then you're in luck, because tonight I am in rare form."

"I can see that." Nic indicated to the pups jockeying for position.

Lucien followed his gaze, and his green eyes glittered with deadly intent. "The problems they present can be easily solved with a quick trip around back."

"Is that what you plan to do later?" Nic asked, eyeing his friend.

"Ah, *mon ami*, I'm a lover, not a fighter. You know that." Lucien winked.

Nic snorted. Lucien was definitely a lover. He *loved* women. Nic had seen him with an endless string of ladies.

One look from the dark-haired, green-eyed Frenchman and women fell to their knees. None of them stayed long, and that suited Lucien just fine. In that respect, they were polar opposites. Nic wanted nothing more than to have a mate to go home to at the end of the day.

As for not being a fighter, there was no way in hell his friend could ever convince him that was the case. The darkness in his green gaze was no illusion. He hadn't come by it from anything other than pain.

"What do you have to do to get a drink around here?" someone shouted.

The muscles in Lucien's arms flexed and his hands tightened on the bar. Lucien's nails lengthened, burrowing into the grainy fibers. Nic heard the wood groan under the pressure.

"You'd better get going, Lover Boy, before the crowd turns on you," Nic said.

Lucien glanced at him. "It wouldn't be the first time." His smile returned, but with a touch of melancholy. *"Au revoir, mon ami."*

# # #
Available Now!

About the Author

Jordan Summers has thirty-one books to her credit and has sold over 135,000 ebooks. She's a member of the Horror Writer's Association, Science Fiction and Fantasy Writers of America, The Author's Guild, and Novelist Inc.

Connect with her online:
Twitter.com/jordanwriter
www.facebook.com/authorjordansummers
https://www.facebook.com/JordanSummersWriter
www.JordanSummers.com
Join the Endless Summers Newsletter to find out about upcoming releases and author signings.
http://www.jordansummers.com/contact/